BY EARTH

THE WITCHES OF PORTLAND, BOOK ONE

T. THORN COYLE

Copyright © 2018
T. Thorn Coyle
PF Publishing

Cover Art and Design © 2018
Lou Harper

Editing:
Dayle Dermatis

ISBN-13: 978-1-946476-05-0

BY EARTH

Haunted by the dead, she fights for the living.

Cassiel thought she had outrun the ghosts, but here they were again, in Portland, Oregon, whispering in her ears.

Between the ghosts and her imminent eviction, Cassie has trouble enough, and then Joe walks into the café…

This is a standalone book in a linked series.
The series can be read in any order.

1

CASSIEL

It was Solstice Eve, the longest night, and the coven had gathered. It was the time that ancient people thought the sun stood still in the sky before reversing itself.

Some said it was the night the sun would be reborn.

So much in her life was uncertain right now; Cassiel welcomed the moment of stillness and the promise of rebirth. Twenty-two years old and healthy, with a pretty enough face and a mass of curly red hair people admired... on the surface, Cassie's life looked pretty good.

Inside, though? She was worried all the time.

The slanted walls of Raquel's attic were painted creamy white, including to the knee walls. The dark planks of the fir floor gleamed in the light from the candles massed on altars in each corner of the space. Nine people sat on bright cushions in a rough circle.

Raquel was not only a coven mate, but Cassiel's boss at the café. A regal black woman with dreadlocks flowing down her back, Raquel looked around the space, making certain everything was ready and in place.

A clap of her hands set a row of metal and beaded

bracelets snapping on her wrists. Two more claps, and Cassiel felt her attention snap itself in place along the column of spine. She felt the rest of the coven exhale around her, and exhaled, too. Ready for magic. Ready for the night.

Raquel gestured toward the center of the room and Moss, a slender Japanese American man in his early twenties, picked up his athame, a double-bladed witch's knife, and began slowly turning in a circle. Cassie felt Moss's blade sweep by her, causing the edges of her skin to prickle and stand at attention.

She could almost see the blue flame she'd been told was the vital energy of magic, and of life itself. Prana. Mana. Essence. She certainly imagined it now, snaking from the blade tip as it traced the edge of the circle.

When he reached the place he had started from, the blade swept up in an arc overhead and then back down, forming a glowing sphere, a sphere of safety, a sphere to focus, a sphere of protection for those within and those without.

Cassie let her soul wander deeper. She let herself open to the magic of the night.

"Cassiel, is your cantrip ready?" Brenda said. The cantrip. The poetry that helped tune magical operations and rituals. Cassie was a poet, and the coven had started looking to her to weave spells of words.

Brenda had been Cassiel's main mentor for the year and a day of her coven apprenticeship. The white woman was in her early forties, with a messy array of brown hair piled on her head. As usual, she wore a flowing tunic over slim pants. Tonight's tunic was black, shot through with purple stars. A chunky silver pendant at her breast reflected the candlelight.

Cassie smoothed her hands on her jeans, tossed the heavy fall of red curls over her shoulder and stood.

Stepping forward to face the north, she said "By earth..." She turned, pointing to each cross quarter in turn, charging up the energy, speaking as she went. "By flame. By wind. By sea. By moon, by sun, by dusk, by dark, by witches' mark..."

Cassie felt the energy build as the words moved through her. They were simple words, but like all magical poetry, their very simplicity increased the potency. What mattered was that they focused the witch's will. What mattered was that they called the planes of existence closer together, joining above and below, within and without.

"...We consecrate this holy ground, with sight, and sound, and breath twined 'round. With will and love, from below to above..."

Cassiel felt as if the whole hub of the cosmos spun around her, within her, and then locked into place. "Let the magic portals open," she said, then stood, vibrating in the hushed, still center of the space for one long breath. Then she bowed and took her place in the circle of the coven once again.

"So mote it be," eight voices responded.

Two other coveners, Alejandro and Lucy, carried a small table and a large black mirror into the center of the circle. The buttoned-up IT guy and the house painter, tall and short. Alejandro saw the future, and Lucy did a lot of work with the ancestors. Those two couldn't have been more different, yet their magic fit together like dusk mirroring dawn.

"Tonight we scry," Raquel said. "We look into the other worlds to see what we can find there. We ask for guidance for the coming year. We ask for help. We ask for visions of what may be, and visions of that which must fall away, and we ask on this, the longest, darkest night, to feel the promise of new light. So mote it be."

Cassie was drifting in and out, between the worlds of matter and æther, feeling the weight of the longest night around her, feeling the magic in the room. She felt a sense of home, as she always did when surrounded by the Arrow and Crescent Coven. She could taste that sense of home, just like she could taste the mulled wine the coven had toasted with before heading up the stairs. The memory of it slept on the back of her tongue.

But she also had to admit the sense of home wasn't as strong as it was before, because even though she still let herself float in the in-between, her anxiety was back.

Cassie watched her coven mates move in and out in groups of two or three to kneel in front of the big black polished mirror, gazing into it, seeking prophecy or reassurance, a way forward or a way to release the past. She realized she was scared—terrified, actually, and growing more frightened by the minute.

The things that were in her past were things she had hoped to keep buried—the ghosts clamoring for her attention, day and night. The inquests. The police calling her for help on cases. Her fourteen-year-old self, shaking and stammering as she tried to testify on a witness stand, testify to things that no one should ever see. To things that no person except murderer and victim should ever know.

Except the victims were ghosts. And Cassiel could see them. Could hear their terrible stories, and see the images of their murders all too clearly in her head.

The ghosts were the reason she fled Tennessee.

"I can't do this," she whispered, "I can't, I can't do this."

Raquel moved towards her, put an arm around her shoulders. Her friend and boss drew Cassie in, and cradled her against her chest for a moment. Then, with a squeeze, she released her and turned Cassie's face toward her with her fingers.

"Cassiel," she murmured softly, "you are a child of the Goddesses and the Gods. You are beloved of this coven, and of the Goddess Diana herself, and we will not forsake you. Whatever it is you see tonight, I will personally help you bear it. You can do this. You got this, girl."

Cassie still felt the tension of sickness clamping down her throat and churning the mulled wine into a sour liquid in her belly as she nodded.

"Guess I'll get it over with," she said.

She moved forward with two other coven mates, Alejandro and her best friend in the coven, the elegant Selene.

She watched as they bowed their heads, gazing into the black expanse, Alejandro's face forming a sharply backlit profile. Selene's face was obscured by a fall of straight black hair. Then she leaned forward herself.

Staring into the black mirror was like staring into the curved bowl of space. Cassiel remembered nights out in the wilderness of Tennessee, coming upon a high place, nothing but black night and stars, so many stars, the kind you couldn't see in the city, the kind of stars she hadn't seen in years. Closing her eyes for a moment, she took three deep breaths and looked once again into the mirror. She saw the glimmering wink of candles, and the dark reflection of her own face. She saw a hand reaching out as though in friendship. She saw her parents. Her grandmother.

Feeling tension rising in her shoulders and belly again, she willed herself to calm down and drew in another deep breath.

"Help me see," she whispered to the mirror, "help me see what I need to see."

All of a sudden the mirror was wiped clean. There was nothing. Just blackness, deep, deep blackness. Cassie leaned in further, trying to keep her eyes soft as they wanted to focus, trying to find anything, something. "Show me, please." And there it was—an image of a burning tower. Cassie gasped and rocked back on her heels.

"No, no, no, no, no," she said.

She felt Raquel next to her. "You're fine, girl. Anoint yourself and look again." Raquel was holding out a small blue bowl of water.

"I don't think I can," Cassie replied.

Raquel was silent, still holding out the bowl. Cassie shook herself, dipped her fingertips into the bowl, then bathed her face and ran damp hands through the top of her hair. She lifted the heavy fall of hair and placed one cool, moist hand on the back of her neck and breathed.

It felt good. "Thank you," she whispered to Raquel, who nodded and moved back again.

Cassiel evened her breathing out and leaned toward the black mirror once again. Her eyes unfocused and Cassiel dropped into the black mirror. She was flying.

Flying through stars, flying through the air, then steering her spirit lower.

She was flying above the city of Portland and then she saw the room that her coven was in—she saw Alejandro and Selene, still kneeling by the black mirror, the other six lying down or sitting in a circle around the altar. She saw that some of them had left their bodies, shimmering silver cords attaching their spirits to their flesh.

She saw her own silvery cord and followed it down. It was as though her spirit were in two places at once, the observer and the observed. Cassie watched herself gazing in the mirror, and felt things go black again.

And then her eyes opened on to the face of a beautiful black woman with the strong, tall body of a warrior, a small tape recorder in one hand and a pen in the other.

"Who are you?" she asked.

"Who I am is not important. I don't exist here anymore, except as memories, ambitions, and work that still needs to be done. I need you to finish it because he can't. He's not able."

"Who? Who can't?"

The woman just shook her head.

"Follow the tower on fire."

"What? I don't understand. What do I need to do?" she asked.

The woman just looked at her with firm eyes, then scribbled something on a piece of paper.

"You will know," the woman said. *"Tell Joe I still love him. And tell Darius I said hi."*

The woman held up the piece of paper. Cassiel peered at it, trying to make out the word.

And then the woman was gone.

2

JOE

*G*asping. *Choking. Sweating.*

That feeling. That feeling something was clawing at him. Feeling like he couldn't escape. He was trapped. He was trapped and he was running.

Joe was running and he was trapped and he didn't know what was happening. He only knew his heart pounded in his chest and his arms were sore from beating at something.

Joe fell to his knees. Wrapped his arms around himself. And he tried...he tried to just. Give up. Tried to just give up, but it wouldn't let him.

It. This nagging, gnawing thing. He couldn't tell if it was inside or outside. But it had him in its grip. The air around him suddenly froze. A big icy finger shot through his heart, filling him with tremors. He shook and shook.

Terrified. He was terrified. But he also felt so sad....

Gasping, Joe woke up with blankets and sheets in a tangle around his legs. His legs felt sore. Bruised.

The sheets were damp with sweat, but Joe was shivering. His room in the beautiful old Craftsman house was freezing.

"What the...?"

The heater in his bedroom must have turned itself off. He couldn't hear the rush of air, or see the glowing red coils in the darkness.

Joe rubbed his hands across his damp face, trying to wake up enough to make sense of what was going on. Then he heard the soft patter of rain on the window and roof.

"The damn electricity must be out again," he murmured, as he struggled into the sweats he'd thrown on top of the quilted blue comforter before he fell asleep.

Joe pulled the tangle of sheets, blanket, and comforter up to his chin, then shrugged and wriggled himself into the cold sweatshirt and sweatpants and a pair of balled-up wool socks. He lay there for a moment, trying to warm up and work up the courage to get out of the damn bed.

It wasn't happening.

"Dang," he said, then finally thought try his bedside lamp.

Click. Click. Sure enough. No light.

"Well...damn!" he said again, and grabbed the flashlight he always kept by his bedside and padded his way down the stairs to the breaker box.

It was just outside the bathroom, down the hall en route to the kitchen.

Snorts and snores let him know he was passing his brother's room as Joe's hand traced itself down the dark hallway wall. He didn't bother with the flashlight yet. His body knew the way, having stumbled downstairs to pee in the darkness many times.

Henry was always snoring. Joe was glad he didn't have to sleep with him, and pitied the woman who ever ended up with his brother long term. She'd have to snore in self-defense. Or get some really good earplugs.

Finally, he reached the downstairs bathroom. Joe blew on his hands.

"It's too damn cold," he muttered. He'd been born and raised in Portland, but his ancestors had also left their mark. For all the ways Joe was an Oregonian through and through, he was still Melanesian and sometimes thought he should go live on a tropical island somewhere. When he had the funds, that was where he took vacation. He loved Fiji, where his family was originally from. Samoa. Belize. Any place but the Portland rain and cold.

Wasn't gonna happen this winter, though. Money was too tight. Joe made great money as a plumber and in the side business rehabbing classic homes with his brother. But the old house they lived in took every bit of extra cash these days. Shoot, they could probably use a roommate to help out, but they were used to each other.

Joe grabbed the icy cold metal handle and opened up the breaker box. Sure enough, there it was. He flipped the switch again. And then realized he should've unplugged the space heater that was probably what caused the problem in the first place.

"Yep, it's that blower that's the culprit," he muttered. A cough came from down the hallway.

Joe should've invested in an electric blanket or one of those radiant heaters. He and Henry had looked at those heaters at Home Repair Mart. They'd bought the fan heater anyway, because it was cheaper. Now they were paying for it. Or he was. Damn Henry's ability to sleep through anything.

Joe hurried, feeling his way back down the hallway and up the wooden stairs that groaned and popped with every step like hundred-year-old wood would do. The creaks escorted him back into his bedroom. The bedside lamp was glowing, the fan whirred, and the heater element coil glowed red.

Joe turned it off and unplugged the thing, then dove back in the bed still fully dressed. This was how it was gonna be until he got another way to heat his room, or until they saved enough money to fix the central heating.

But forget about that for now. No way did they have the cash for that big a job. "*We got to do it right, bro*," his brother said, meaning putting central heat and air in at the same time.

Joe knew he was right, but he didn't like it much. He sighed and went to turn the bedside lamp out before realizing he needed the warmth of the light. The sense of being chased still lingered.

Darkness would bring sleep and sleep would bring the dream again.

Maybe if he laid here, hoodie pulled tight around his face, and thought for a while, he could figure it out. Figure out why it kept showing up, once a month, freaking him out and leaving him short of sleep. This had been going on for the past year and a half. Not that long after Tarika died.

Sure enough, just *starting* to think about it, the dream resurged, tapping at his head.

At first the dream felt as if he was chasing after something. The therapist he saw for the first six months after Tarika died thought he was trying to pursue her spirit somehow. Trying to bring her back to a place that felt safe. Not frightening.

A place that felt like home. Real home. Not a place where she felt so alone she couldn't even confess that she had intended to kill herself, let alone go through with it.

But then, three months after Joe gave up on therapy, the dream changed. Instead of running *after* something, something was running after him. He hated it. It freaked him out worse than anything in his life.

He tried to talk to Henry about it, but his brother wasn't any more help than the therapist.

"Maybe you should ask Raquel," Henry had said. "Isn't she psychic or some shit?"

Joe felt too stupid to ask Raquel. He felt too stupid about a lot of things. Maybe that was what the dream was about. He always felt bruised and battered lately. Though since Tarika killed herself, he didn't so much feel like he was running as hiding.

If he could have curled up in a shell, he would have.

That had finally started to change, just a few months ago. Joe was finally feeling more like himself. Business was good. He liked working on projects with Henry. He was going out for drinks with the guys.

But he hadn't started dating, that was for sure, despite his brother bugging him about it. Joe hadn't looked at a woman since Tarika died. Not really. Not that way.

So why was the dream back now? What was trying to get his attention?

His therapist had said it was his subconscious, working through the helplessness and grief.

Now Joe wasn't so sure.

He wasn't so sure the dream was anything inside of him at all.

It felt too real.

It felt like it was outside, and chasing after him.

Joe just wasn't sure yet whether or not the thing meant him any harm.

But something sure was on his tail.

3

CASSIEL

Cassiel had a job. Poetry. A coven she loved.

But pretty soon she was going to be out of a home. And the ghosts had held themselves at bay so far, after two years of her running as far and fast from them as possible.

They hadn't appeared in her dreams, or out of the blue on a sunny day, needing help, screaming about death. There had been no calls from the police, asking her to come look at a crime scene and tell them if "she could pick anything up" from the empty, terrifying rooms.

It was December 20th, Solstice morning, and also a Monday. The café was thankfully warm and snug from the combination of the heater working overtime, the panini grill that had been popping out hot breakfast sandwiches all morning, and the steamer on the gleaming espresso machine.

There wasn't enough coffee in the world to help Cassiel keep up. She and Raquel were both bleary-eyed from the ritual the night before. No one else had been available to open the café, and Solstice occurred when Solstice occurred. Schedules be damned.

It was really cold outside, frost on the windows, so close to freezing that Cassie wondered if it was going to snow. She actually hoped so. It didn't snow very often in Portland, so when it hit, it was kind of magic.

Cassiel needed more of that sort of magic. Yeah, magic had felt in pretty short supply lately. And last night's ritual, which should have helped, had just left her feeling unsettled. That woman and her messages...she'd had the scent of ghost about her, but Cassie wasn't sure.

Or she didn't want to be sure.

She wiped down the counter and then headed for the red Naugahyde booths lined up along the wall. The café was quiet, just some early Smiths on low, Morrissey complaining about his loneliness again. The morning rush had just ended, so she was catching up on cleaning while her boss, Raquel, restocked some of the food before the café lunch crowd hit.

Wiping down a table that had recently held her favorite lesbian couple and their two kids, she scrubbed at a particularly stubborn spot with a wet rag. The table was sticky with grape jelly from toasted peanut butter sandwiches. Toasted peanut butter and jelly actually sounded pretty good right now. Comfort food.

Frankly, after last night's visions, she needed a little comfort. That taste in your mouth that signaled someone cared enough about you to make your favorite food. Something simple. Something a little sweet and a little nourishing.

Stop it. Cassie. You've got work to do.

A customer walked in the door, letting in a blast of frigid air and the scent of cold and car exhaust. Cassie hurried back behind the counter, throwing her rag in a bucket of water laced with orange peel essence.

"Hello, may I help you?"

A white woman in her mid-twenties with a round beautiful face, round like the moon, smiled across the counter, spikes of black hair peeking out from beneath a burgundy knit cap. A heavy messenger bag was slung across her chest. Her cheeks and the tip of her rounded nose were tinged with pink from the cold. She had on a black wool coat and fingerless burgundy gloves that matched the hat.

"What can I get for you?"

"Cappuccino, please, with coconut milk. And..." The woman looked up at the chalkboard hanging behind Cassie, perusing her options. "Could I get a bagel with ham?"

"What's your name?" Cassie asked, as she rang her up and made change for the crumpled twenty the woman pulled from her coat pocket.

"Olivia."

"Great, Olivia, I'll have that cappuccino up in just a minute."

Cassie watched her sit down at one of the booths she'd just cleaned and drag a laptop from the messenger bag. Scooping out some freshly ground espresso, Cassie tamped it into the portafilter, inhaling in appreciation. She'd already had two coffees this morning. No more allowed.

Everyone came to Raquel's to work. Especially after the rush was over and the space cleared out, like the two writers at the corner table. Regulars. Tall soy latte and a regular coffee. Sometimes they split a danish. They were typing away, the black woman on a novel, and the the white guy? Probably working on some article he had due if he was on deadline, or on the novel he worked on in between assignments.

Cassie slammed the filter into the group head and yanked the handle tight.

She envied that pair of writers. Story was that they'd met a few years previous during National Novel Writing Month and had been coming to Raquel's three days a week ever since, without fail. Apparently, both of them made decent money.

Waiting for the espresso machine to start spitting the brown gold from its spouts, she got the coconut milk from the little fridge below the long counter. That was what she should do. Learn how to write novels.

No money in poetry, that was for sure. Not that money was really Cassie's current problem. Her problem was the shifting landscape of a city with a fairly temperate climate and a constant fresh influx of tenants, and zero rent control.

And greedy developers and landlords.

Yeah. A landlord raising her rent by fifty percent practically overnight was not a money problem. It was a greed problem.

Cassie sighed. She never thought she'd become some sort of radical. Still wasn't. Not like Moss, in her coven. She just wanted to live her life and write beautiful things.

Cassie loved poetry. Always had. People said she had a way with words. She got that from her mother, just like the pale white skin that burned in seconds as soon as the sun emerged. Other inheritances? Long, tapered fingers which meant she should've played piano. Or basketball. And the huge mass of red-orange hair currently piled up on her head.

She liked to wear it down but never could do that at work because hair got everywhere. In sponges. On the floor. Tucked around the edges of plates.

Clearing the vacuum cleaner at home was a constant

chore, and she had to get one of those special hair traps in the shower, otherwise the shower and sink would be constantly clogged. Speaking of which.

"Hey, isn't that plumber coming today?" Cassie asked Raquel. Raquel's dreadlocks were tied back to in a purple scarf that matched the purple moon-and-star–patterned sweater she wore over dark blue denim jeans. She was somewhere around thirty-five years old, if Cassie was guessing, but frankly, with witches it was always hard to tell.

Raquel held a clear plastic container of onions and one of sliced red bell peppers, which she put in their slots under the metal hood behind the counter.

"Yep. My neighbor Joe is coming in. I hope he can fix it. It's a pain in the ass the way that thing's leaking. I would fix it myself, but don't have the time."

At least they didn't have to shut the bathroom down. Luckily it wasn't that bad, but the thing kept leaking every time someone washed their hands and it was Cassie's job to go empty the bucket in between.

"Can you make a sandwich?"

"On it," Raquel replied, glancing at the ticket Cassie'd shoved into the bar above the work counter. She sliced a plain bagel in half and threw it on one of the rotating toaster racks.

The smell of warming yeast filled the air, mingling with the scents of caffeine, along with ham and cheese from the array of breakfast sandwiches they'd been hustling all morning to make on the panini press.

Cassie put the metal pitcher under the steam wand and began bringing the coconut milk to a froth.

She had already poured the double shot of espresso into one of the red cups that were a signature of the cafe. Cassie poured the milk in, layer by layer. The trick was to make a perfect series of circles, and then drag the final pour up through the center, forming a heart.

That was always so satisfying. Cassie wanted to learn to make fancier shapes, but had never taken the time.

"What's happening with your housing? Any luck?" Raquel asked.

"No, not yet. It looks like I'm going to lose my place. I can't pay the increase, and when I called the Tenants Union, they said the only thing I can do right now is refuse to pay in protest as a way to buy more time. I don't know what I'm going to do."

"Something will happen," Raquel said. "I believe that. I can feel it in my bones."

Raquel was clairsentient. That meant she got psychic information through her body.

Cassie just hoped she was right. Wow. Did she need something.

"Well, I'm going to an actual Tenants Union meeting later this week. We'll see if they've got more ideas."

"They're good people," Raquel said. "They tried to help my family years ago."

"Your family?" Cassie really needed to get the coffee out to Olivia, but wanted to hear this.

"Yep. We used to live up northeast, 'til we got pushed out by gentrification."

Raquel buttered the warm bagel and began layering thinly sliced ham on top.

"That's where it started, you know. No one with money wanted to live down here in felony flats with all the white, meth-dealing gangs, but they sure could push working class black folks out of our homes up in the north part of the city."

"Damn," Cassie said. "Got to get this cappuccino out."

"Take the bagel, too. It's done."

Olivia was working on spreadsheets, earbuds plugged into her ears. She smiled and mouthed a thank you as Cassie set her late breakfast down.

Cassie wondered what it would be like. To come work in a café. Use it as your office instead of working at the café. Maybe she'd find out some day—though, yeah, as long as she kept calling herself a poet, it seemed unlikely. And if she didn't find a place she could afford, who knew how long she'd even be in Portland?

A recent arrival, Cassie was getting pushed out like everyone else.

The door opened again, letting in a blast of frigid air.

A young man with dark brown hair pulled back in a bun walked in. He had pale brown skin and a goatee. Stamping big work boots on the industrial rug in the doorway, he unzipped a heavy, quilt-lined work coat.

The black swoop of a tattoo peeked out from the top of a navy thermal shirt.

Cassie felt a rush of attraction run through her whole body. The man was seriously cute. More than cute, even.

He caught Cassie's eye and then immediately looked down at the floor.

Huh. Okay, he was cute, but kind of weird. And just because her body responded to someone, didn't mean she couldn't control her thoughts.

Cassie didn't have time for men anyway. There was more work to do, and she *really* had to find a place to live.

4

JOE

Joe stamped his tan work boots on the industrial carpet just inside the heavy glass café door. The usual bright art, this time from a local printmaker, hung from the walls, and the delicious combination of roasted coffee beans and hot panini sandwiches filled the air.

Hooo, it was still cold out, temperature dropping low enough to actually snow. If it did, Joe hoped it wouldn't last too long. He just wasn't built for that kind of cold.

He hadn't been in Raquel's in months. He made his morning coffee at home and the place was always too busy during lunch to bother coming by.

A young woman was behind the counter, skin pale like moonlight, her wavy hair in an amazing shade of red piled up on top of her head. She was strong-jawed for such a delicate frame. And she was gorgeous.

Seriously beautiful. It made him want to run back out the door in panic. He just wasn't good with women.

And he hadn't looked at anyone that way since Tarika died.

Henry would smack the back of his head if he knew. They'd had that conversation already.

"Tarika was great, bro, but you dated for what? Two years? And she's been dead a year and a half..." As though there were some set equation for grief. Or guilt.

Even so, Joe couldn't help but wonder what that mass of red hair looked like when it was down instead of bunched up on top of her head like a luminous pineapple. Oh God. He was gonna have to talk to her, wasn't he?

Whipping his head around, he didn't see Raquel anywhere. Just folks working at tables, cups of coffee close at hand. This was so not good. Joe forced himself to not wipe his hands on his pants, and unzipped his heavy jacket instead. Damn his social anxiety.

Yep. He was gonna have to talk to her. *Okay, just do it Joe. She's not gonna bite you.*

"Raquel here?" he asked, and then she smiled. Oh no. He couldn't even look at her. Beautiful women like her? No way. Joe was the comic book geek, nose always buried in Superman, X-Men, Hulk, anything he could get his hands on. Aquaman... Always a favorite.

It didn't even help when he started skateboarding. Joe thought that would up his cool quotient, like it did with some of the other dudes. The girls didn't seem to care. All they saw was his awkwardness. Plus, he was still a little too skinny despite the muscles he put on working as a plumber and general handyman.

Joe exhaled with relief as Raquel came out from the back just then, carrying several heavy bags of coffee beans, dreadlocks tied back, exposing that pretty dark face of hers, with full lips and high cheekbones.

"Hey Joe. Cold enough? Can I get you a coffee?" she

asked, after handing off the bags of beans to the younger woman.

Raquel was great. She'd really helped him and his brother out since they bought the house four years ago. She had a good eye for design, and had even suggested they put a wall up in the attic, to make the space up there more usable.

She also let them borrow her lawnmower during the summer months and invited them over for a beer when they'd been working hard on the house all day. All in all, she was pretty dope.

"Yeah, sure. I wouldn't mind one. Regular."

She pumped coffee into a big red cup from one of the thermal carafes they kept on counter and handed it over.

It felt good in his hands, warming up his cold fingers. He really should be wearing gloves, but hadn't figured the short walk from his truck would be that bad.

Joe went to the side table that held coffee condiments and doctored his mug with a little raw sugar and some cream.

"So, you want to come on back and take a look before you grab your tools?" Raquel asked.

Joe nodded again and followed after Raquel, heading down the short hallway to the back, trying not to check out her backside, focusing instead on the neat dreadlocks that flowed down her back. Henry was a dog. Joe tried his best not to be.

He could never tell how old she was. Just like with other darker skinned folks—Pacific Islanders like his family. They looked the same for years. They stayed young looking until all of a sudden something changed and they didn't anymore.

"How long has it been acting up?" He remembered the cup warming up his hands was good for more than a hand warmer. It actually had coffee in it. He took a sip. Good as always.

"Pssh. A few days," Raquel said. "I would've fixed it myself but I just don't have time. Besides, I figure I'd try you out. See if you're any good."

She shot Joe a grin, teeth white against her dark skin.

I'm probably too young for her. Which was too bad, because he actually felt comfortable around her, which was not the way it usually was. Besides, Raquel was a friend and needed to stay that way. At least that was what he told himself.

He was such a damn nerd.

Raquel had never shown any inclination toward him other than friendship, and no way was Joe going to push something with a woman who was also his neighbor. Not unless a mutual attraction was clear.

The washroom was big enough to be ADU compliant. There was a storage cabinet in the corner nearest the door, a rolling cart, the grab bar by the toilet and sink, and a large chalkboard along the back wall.

Someone had gone to town on that recently. The black board was a marvel of colored chalk: blues, whites, and purples swirling together in a cloud with a face on one end, blowing up a storm.

"Okay, let's see," he said. Setting his mug on the rolling cart that held extra toilet paper, he opened the cabinet underneath the sink. Sure enough, there was a drip bucket under the sink trap, and all the cleaning supplies had been shoved to one side. He caught a whiff of orange peel solvent and bleach.

"And?" Raquel asked.

Joe raised his head and looked at her furrowed brow.

"Don't sweat it, neighbor. It looks simple enough but I won't know until I take it all apart. I'll go get my toolbox."

Joe brushed his heavy work pants off as he climbed up off the black-and-white linoleum.

Raquel leaned against the door frame, arms crossed over her chest. "You know anyone that has a place for rent? Not too expensive?"

"Not really," Joe replied. "I mean, Henry and I talk about it sometimes, but I don't know anyone who would want to live in our house and have us banging and sawing every weekend. Why do you ask?"

"Cassiel needs a place. She's getting kicked out. Forced eviction. Raised her rent practically double."

"It's happening all over, isn't it?" he said as they walked out toward the front of the café.

"Yep. Rich folks taking over everywhere. Coming in from out of town. Buying stuff up, squeezing people out."

"California money," he said.

"California money," Raquel replied.

"But I guess they're moving here 'cause it's cheaper then where they're from. Right?"

"That doesn't make it feel any better."

"No. It doesn't. Be right back," Joe said.

He glanced toward the cash register. The red-haired woman was looking at him again. He ducked his head, zipped his coat up, and headed back outside.

After making his way across the icy sidewalk to his battered old orange Ford, Joe unlocked the fancy metal chest at the rear of the truck bed.

His phone buzzed in his pocket. No message. No calls.

Weird. He felt a tingle on his cheek and looked up, expecting snow. Just dark clouds. No rain, no snow. Something in that ghost of a touch felt both strange and familiar. As though it was a close cousin to a touch he'd felt before.

He placed a hand on his cheek. Damn, he did need gloves. His hands were freezing. Then he looked back at his phone. Still no message.

Joe shrugged and grabbed his medium-sized red toolbox in his freezing right hand, then relocked the big chest.

Back in the café, he nodded at the young woman behind the counter. She must be Cassiel.

Cassiel was a beautiful name. Name of an angel.

"Need another coffee?" she asked him.

He gave her a slight smile, then looked back down at his toolbox. "Maybe when I'm done," he said, and kept going.

He walked down the short hallway to the bathroom, clunked the toolbox down, and slid to the linoleum floor.

"Joe, you have got to get your shit together," he said, staring at the pipes beneath the sink.

Then he brought out the big, scarred-up red pipe wrench, and got to work.

5

CASSIEL

I t was literally freezing outside by the time Cassie got off work at the café, but her friend and coven mate Selene wanted tacos, so Cassie bundled her pile of red hair into a wool hat, wrapped a scarf around her neck, and made the trek to the Mercado.

The lug soles of her boots periodically crunched over ice. Last night's rain now lay frozen in patches on the sidewalks.

The Mercado was an outdoor row of brightly painted Latin American food trucks that had the best burritos and tacos in town. There was even Haitian or Puerto Rican food if you were looking for it, but Cassie was partial to blue corn soft tacos.

It was right near the café, so a convenient place to meet, considering she didn't have a car. However, Cassie insisted that they not sit at the big tables outside.

"Are you crazy? It's got to be below forty!" she said. "You damn Wisconsinite, I bet you think this is warm. My Tennessee blood can't handle this."

Selene just smiled and shrugged shoulders encased in a

black wool coat, deep hood framing their pale, luminous face.

So, food in hand, they crowded into the little wine and beer restaurant, with an amber pint of IPA in front of Cassie and a glass of Pinot Noir for Selene.

Selene was always more upscale like that. Wine instead of beer. They looked great as usual. Perfectly plucked black eyebrows and a swoop of black eyeliner framing green eyes. Pale foundation smoothing out the nonexistent flaws in their skin. Ruby stain on their lips.

Selene had fled their family in Wisconsin years ago, which was why they didn't mind the cold. They always wore makeup and always dressed just so, in a mildly androgynous Goth sort of way. Today was no exception. The black wool coat. White shirt buttoned up to the neck, with what looked like at least ten silver necklaces over it. Loose black cardigan.

Doc Marten boots were the one concession to the fact that it had rained recently, and that rain very well might turn to ice or snow.

And Selene's fingernails always had flecks of paint marring their polish, and Cassie could see they'd missed a couple of spots while washing up. Blue and green splotches danced across blunt fingers.

They could've sat at one of the long counters in the main part of the building, where there were a couple of stores selling Mexican groceries, a pretty extensive butcher counter, and some shops selling goods from Central America, but the bar was cozy. Cassie liked it.

She hadn't tried the butcher shop yet. Probably should someday.

Taking a bite of the vegetarian taco, Cassiel scrambled to keep it from falling apart. The soft blue corn tortilla barely held itself together around the winter squash and spinach mingled with the onions, salsa, and radishes.

"Goddess, this is good," she practically moaned. The pulled pork taco she'd already chowed down on was equally good.

"Speaking of good, how's your love life?" Selene asked.

Cassie grimaced. "I could ask you the same."

Selene took the opportunity to delicately stuff another bite of burrito into their face. Selene always avoided the love conversation. There'd been a bad breakup a year ago and Selene had been flying solo ever since.

Cassie couldn't understand how Selene could eat so much. Selene was a regular CrossFit beast, as they liked to call themself, so Cassie supposed they needed all those calories, but Cassie could never fit more than half a burrito in her belly. That was truly a pity, because they were good too.

"I did meet a cute plumber today. He came in to the café to fix the bathroom sink. Neighbor of Raquel's. Super cute. But super shy. He barely looked at me, so I doubt it'll go anywhere."

They ate in silence for a minute.

"So, you got any leads?" Selene asked when they finally slowed down on the burrito enough to take another sip of wine.

"No," Cassie sighed, setting down her taco. Her hands dripped with salsa runoff. Grabbing a brown paper napkin from the pile she'd gotten outside, she wiped at her hands, ripping the paper in the process.

"I actually don't know what I'm gonna do," Cassie said. "I may end up couch surfing for a couple months until I can find a place. And if I really can't find a place, I may have to move out of town."

She took a sip of beer. Gah. Part of her wanted to just drink until she drowned.

"You can't leave us!" Selene said. "You can't leave the coven, and your friends, and everything else...."

The tacos felt like a lump inside Cassie's stomach. Selene was right. She'd just finished her year and a day with the coven and was finally a full, active participant. It felt as though she maybe even had a chance to learn something. Something real.

It also felt like her chance to set the past to rest. Finally. But of course, now the universe was conspiring to take it all away again. As long as the ghosts didn't come back, she'd make it through. She hoped.

"I don't want to go, but I don't see...don't know what to do. I've been trying with the Tenants Union, and even petitioned my landlord, but nothing's budging. I'm just like every other marginally poor person in this city. Screwed."

"We'll find you someplace. Have you asked the Gods?"

Cassie shook her head, sure she was staring at Selene as if she didn't know what they were talking about. Selene shook her head.

"Why not? Like, that's basic. You *have* done magic about this situation, right, Cassiel?"

Cassie just sat there, then picked up the rest of her veggie taco.

"Cassie?"

She sighed. Damn it. She wasn't used to people seeing her like this. Or calling her on her shit.

"I don't trust my magic yet," she admitted. "I feel like I'm going to screw it up." Or as if it was going to backfire on her, badly. Or she'd end up the center of a bunch of unwanted attention again.

"Oh girlfriend, please, we have *got* to get you doing some magic and we have got to do that *now.*"

They ate in silence for a moment, listening to the Tejano music being piped through the Mercado while Selene clearly plotted out some plan in their head.

They took another sip of wine, training those beautiful eyes on Cassie over the rim of the glass. Uh oh. Cassie felt like an insect in a glass cabinet. Or as if every single one of her emotions was on display. And in front of Selene? They probably were.

"Cassie, I'm not going to read you, and I don't want to pry, but I can tell something is wrong. Like...there's something you're not telling me. It's obvious you're powerful, so what gives? Why *not* trust your magic?"

Ugh. First the tacos, then the beer turned sour in Cassie's stomach. She set the taco remnants down.

"I can't talk about it."

A flash of hurt crossed her friend's face before Selene shrugged and took another sip of wine.

"I said I wouldn't pry."

"It's just...I'm not ready to talk about it. Not yet. I'm..." Cassie looked out the window. The snow was starting to fall. A gorgeous, soft drift of flakes moved through the lights of the Mercado, heading toward the paved brick ground. *I'm afraid,* she thought. But she was also too afraid to even voice the words.

"What are you doing tonight?" Selene finally asked.

Cassie turned back toward Selene and managed a small smile. "Magic?"

"Magic," Selene replied. "Finish your tacos. We're going back to your place after we swing by mine for some supplies."

"How do you know I don't have what we need?"

"Because if you did, and didn't already use it? I'd have to kick your ass." Selene's smile lit up the room. The only thing they liked more than art was magic.

As Cassie smiled back at her friend and took another sip of beer, she realized something around her felt a little lighter. To be honest, Selene always had that effect. It was their gift. A gift with a capital G.

Selene was an empath. Cassie knew that was hard on them sometimes, but it sure did help the people around them feel better.

Cassie gauged her stomach. Still a little sour, but also still hungry.

She started in on the third and last taco.

6

JOE

J oe had never been a guy who complained about his
problems much. Matter of fact, for most of his life
until Tarika died, he'd never been a guy who felt as if
he had that many problems at all.

But lately, things weren't going great and he wasn't sure
what to do about it.

Henry was out and about somewhere, probably trying to
pick up on some women. His brother was a great guy, even
though he went through women faster than Joe would ever
be comfortable with. He'd offered to let Joe tag along, but
Joe needed to think.

Joe sat in the mostly empty living room space in his
favorite old worn gray leather recliner. The fireplace needed
fixing, like everything in the place, so the hearth was cold.
Joe liked sitting next to the fireplace anyway. It was one of
his favorite features of the old house, with a green cracked
glaze tile surround. The central tile was an elaborate
painted tile showing boats on the Columbia River.

His chair was comfortable, designed to be sat in for
hours at a time. It was one of those pieces of furniture that

cost more than he made in six months. And he'd gotten it for free. Well, actually, he'd gotten it for labor. This old, formerly rich dude had needed help moving a bunch of stuff out of his mansion. He'd lost it all in the stock market crash and had to downsize. One of the things he offered Joe as payment for his help was this amazing chair.

It was Joe's thinking chair. His reading chair. It was his sipping-on-a-beer-when-he-needed-to-ponder-things-alone chair.

And that was what he was doing now. With a Negra Modelo in one hand, and his chin in the other. The mystery of Tarika's death had bothered him ever since it happened. It wasn't just the chest-crushing grief of having her gone. It wasn't just dealing with her irate brother, who somehow blamed Joe for her death. It was that suicide didn't make any *sense*.

Tarika had been so *alive*. She was gorgeous and funny. She was a brilliant reporter with a great job with the *Mount Tabor Monthly*, the only newspaper in town doing in-depth stories on local topics instead of just reporting the police blotter, occasional human-interest fluff, or a rehash of global news off the wires. She was healthy, and he thought they were in love. At least that was what she had told him.

And, really more importantly, that was what it had felt like. Joe could always feel that Tarika loved him.

It was one of the things that he missed about her. Not just her amazing life, but the way she made him feel. No one had ever made Joe feel loved like that. Not his parents. Not his friends. Not the other girls and women he dated over the years.

With Tarika he finally had a sense of home. A sense of belonging. He wasn't sure anyone else would ever make him feel that way.

"God. I thought I was over this," he said, swigging more of the dark beer.

Thought he was over the crushing-ness of it. Thought he was over trying to solve the mystery of it. But clearly he wasn't.

Just when he'd been ready to move on, all the feelings would come rushing back again. So here he was. Alone in his chair. His brother worried about him. Hence tonight's invitation.

"I'll be fine," Joe had said. So his brother had reluctantly left him alone. Men were good that way. They knew when to push and when to stop pushing. His brother was especially good with that. With giving a guy his space. That was why they could work together and share a house without killing one another.

The beer was a little sour in his mouth. Hoppy. Rich. Joe wished he had some tortilla chips to go with it, maybe some salsa, but they were all the way in the kitchen, and he was firmly ensconced, his butt already forming to the ridges in the chair made by all the hours he'd sat there on his own.

Joe knew Tarika had been working on something before she killed herself. That was the other thing that didn't make sense. Once Tarika got a thing in her teeth, she didn't let it go. So why in the world would she make sure she couldn't finish a story? But everything pointed to suicide. Pills in her system. Her favorite brand of rum.

And they couldn't find anything missing. Joe had immediately asked them to check. To see if it looked like her computer had been wiped. If there were missing files. Joe sat up straighter, frowning. He thought he felt something. Like the feeling you got when someone was watching you.

There was definitely something weird in the room. He looked around. No one was there. Just him and a single lamp plugged into an unprotected socket, waiting for the baseboards to be put back in and a plate to be installed. One of the tiny little finish work projects that they weren't going to get to until the major work was done.

Besides, in a house this old? You heard every single footstep. No way anyone could sneak up on a person in a hundred-year-old Craftsman. *Something* was bothering him, though. He got up and shut the green curtains on the night. He didn't trust that someone wasn't outside looking in.

There wouldn't have been any files on her computer, he realized. Shit. Of course. He *knew* that. But he hadn't thought it through before.

He hadn't thought much through. The grief that had punched him repeatedly in the chest didn't leave much room for rational thought.

Besides, Joe just didn't work with computers enough to even think about it. He barely used them, just to answer the e-mails from his clients. Computers were just a way to keep in touch with people who wanted to hire Mara Brothers to rehab their old houses.

Joe worked with his hands all day. He wasn't one of those Facebook and Twitter people. He wasn't Instagram man. Except, well, Henry had insisted their company get an Instagram account recently—Facebook, too—so they could post photos of their projects. It was a good idea, but Joe still hated it.

"But Tarika," he whispered. She was a computer person. She was also paranoid.

Tarika would have kept it all on thumb drives. Every story. Right. She told him that once. He remembered. They'd been out, on the river pathway. She wouldn't have sensitive conversations in her home. That was how paranoid she was. He'd forgotten that, though. It had been too long.

The events that had come between then and now had stolen huge chunks of memory and time.

They'd been walking next to the Willamette River one summer evening. It was beautiful out. The wind ruffled the beautiful, dark tight curls of her hair. He had his arm around her muscular waist, with just the right amount of softness over the top. Her luscious, strong, curvy body.

"Size 16 and proud," she'd always say.

"Size 16 and smokin' hot," he would always reply.

God, he missed her.

But he'd asked her, after his computer crashed and he lost a bunch of customer files, what she did about that. He always printed everything out and backed it up on paper. She laughed and said that was a good idea. She did that sometimes too. Keeping important pieces of information and contacts in a fire safe vault. But what she mostly did was just back things up on a series of coded thumb drives.

"Where did those thumb drives go?" he wondered. The thing about the thumb drives was, there was no way to tell what was missing and what wasn't. Only Tarika would have known.

He finished his beer and was just contemplating heading to the kitchen for another when the green curtains ruffled and the air near the window started to shimmer.

"What?" he said.

And there she was, with her flaming red hair, a slight furrow in her beautiful pale brow. That woman from the café. What was her name?

Some weird angel name. Cassiel.

She was almost the opposite of Tarika. Cassiel was small and slender, where Tarika was an Amazon. Cassiel had pale skin instead of dark, and bright red hair instead of chestnut brown. But there was something about her that had drawn him in all the same, the minute he set eyes on her in Raquel's café.

It must have been her spirit. He loved complex women, Tarika was proof of that, and Cassiel seemed like she had a lot going on beneath the surface.

But how in the hell was he seeing her here? Now?

The vision furrowed a brow, then smiled and reached for him.

Joe gasped, his heart pounding and his mouth flooded with spit. He was afraid.

"What are you doing here?" he asked. "How?"

She stopped reaching and held up one pale hand...and then she was gone.

"Oh my God I'm losing it. Holy shit." Joe sat, panting for awhile, then heaved himself from the embrace of the leather chair and went to the kitchen to grab another beer, and those tortilla chips.

He wasn't going to get to sleep anytime soon. Not after whatever the hell that was.

7

CASSIEL

Selene's attic apartment was just as spooky-looking as
Selene was. It was small and comfortable like Cassie's
place, but Cassiel felt like she'd need to be a much more
interesting person than she was in order to live in a place
like this.

Then again, she'd had enough of interesting in her own
life for a while. It was kind of a relief to skirt the edges of
normalcy, even though she knew that normal was a lie.

The old scarred wood floors were scattered with jewel-
toned rugs. The queen-size bed in the corner had a dark
walnut slatted headboard and was draped with a comforter
of burgundy and gold.

A jutting dormered area had three windows that looked
out onto a towering fir. Cassie could barely make out the
lamp across the street through the needles and branches.
The area held an easel with a sketched-in canvas on it, a
rack for finished paintings, and drawers and low cabinets
that must have held art supplies. A drop cloth covered
the floor.

The rest of the open apartment space was dedicated to

art and books. Large acrylic paintings, small oils, prints. And one small sculpture of a woman with a bird's head, arms upraised, tiny conical breasts bared.

Cassie was still nervous, but had to admit that part of her was looking forward to doing *something* that might help. She plopped down on a comfortable easy chair covered with a black sheet, facing its companion and a low, round wood table. An empty wine glass with a smear of red lipstick on the rim and the washed-out, purple-red dregs of wine in the bottom sat next to a small stack of books.

"I've never even asked how long you've been a witch," Cassie said.

"I've been a witch since as long as I can remember, practically," Selene said, fussing with tea things in a kitchen as small as Cassiel's own. "My father tended herbs and gardened all the time. It was the only thing that kept him sane in his sales job. And I grew up kind of psychic, though no one talked about it much. Chamomile okay?"

"Yeah, thanks. So, I've never done this kind of magic before. I'm not sure exactly what I should be doing. How does this stuff work?"

Selene brought over a tray laden with a squat green pot and two mismatched mugs. Cassie could smell the grassy chamomile, with slight tinge of lavender, rising from the steam.

"Well, there's a long history of people doing magic for justice," Selene said. "Mostly oppressed people. There are a lot of hoodoo spells for it, and stories about people coming to witches in Ireland for help battling landlords. I should tell you those sometime."

They poured tea into the mugs and handed one to Cassie. The tea was good. Soothing. Cassie needed soothing.

"I've only ever done magic for basic things. Like to find a place to live. And a job."

"And how'd that work?"

"Worked out great. It hooked me up with the coven, which got me the job at Raquel's café."

Magic really *had* worked. It was kind of amazing to her. When she was a kid, she always *hoped* magic was real. She loved playing let's pretend. It was never about princesses, or knights, or even astronauts. It was always about witches and wizards. Or the ability to fly without machines. Or the ability to go to strange places in the blink of an eye.

As she got older, she just went underground with it. She started reading fantasy novels in which good triumphed and the bad wizard always lost in the end.

And then the freaky ghosts-showing-up and police-asking-for-help stuff happened and it all got out of control. Cassie shoved that thought aside. The bad wizard wasn't going to win this round without a fight. Cassie exhaled.

"So, tell me what do I need to do."

"We can use the waning moon we're in to banish the obstacles that stand in the way of justice and to help us see the things that are hidden in the darkness."

"Okay, that makes sense," Cassie said. "I think I get it."

"It's kind of like the using the scrying mirror. The black mirror shows you all the faces you don't see in the light of day."

Selene got up and walked over to a big old cedar chest sitting under a window. They opened the big hinged lid and drew out a smaller wooden box.

"Here're some herbs that will be useful. High John is very good for justice. It's traditional. A lot of spells use this. You can use it if you ever have a court case, or you can just use it in general to bring people to justice."

"What else would we use?"

Selene brought the box over and sat back down. They opened the lid and a bunch of strange, pungent smells emerged, battling with the chamomile tea Cassie still clutched in her hands.

Selene rustled and rummaged and finally drew several packets out, setting them on the table.

"The other thing you need to decide," they said, "is what kind of candle to use. What color? White to bring hidden things to light. Black to banish. Or you could use green for earth, which relates to your home."

"Well, I think I want to bring things to light because I'm not sure yet what I need to banish other than this sucky situation. I don't have enough clarity. You need clarity to do a banishing, right?"

Selene nodded.

"Let's use wolfsbane for protection."

"You think I need that?"

Selene arched one of their perfectly plucked and painted black eyebrows. "You are about to lose your home. But you don't think you need protection?"

Well, put that way, Cassiel guessed she did.

"So, wolfsbane and High John the Conqueror root, a candle, and the power of the moon. Simple," they said.

"Thank you so much, Selene. I've just been at my wits' end. When I left home, I said I was always going to make my way, and I *have* been. But lately I've wondered if I needed to run back with my tail between my legs."

"That's not going to happen," Selene said. "We're going to get you through this."

Cassie exhaled, trying to release the tension again. "What now?"

"Hold the root in your left hand and the wolfsbane in

your right. Just for a moment. As long as you feel you need to."

Cassie picked up the gnarled little root that looked like a dried-up fig, or a turd, and took a pinch of the small dried green leaves from the small pile on the altar.

"Think about justice and what justice means to you. Think about home. And what home means to you."

Cassie did that, breathing deeply. She thought about her anger, and her frustration at the lack of justice. She saw all the people sleeping in tents under the freeway overpasses. And the people she saw on the street sometimes outside the café. She thought of her landlord. "Show me," she said. "Show me, what does justice mean?"

Justice felt like things in the universe being put right again. Justice felt like a big balance, shifting like weighted scales. Adjusting to a state that didn't even have to be perfectly even, but just more equal than it was now. And what did home feel like? Home felt like a place to rest. A place to laugh. A place to study. Maybe even a place to fall in love. Refuge.

Everyone needed a refuge. Too many people didn't have one.

She opened her eyes.

"Got it?" Selene asked.

"I think so."

"Good. Set down the root, but keep the wolfsbane. I want you to rub the dried leaves on the white taper. Make sure you swipe toward your body."

"To draw the protection toward me?"

"Right."

Cassie did, feeling the dried leaves crumble as she pressed them out and upward across the wax. She found herself rocking back and forth as she did. Rocking forward, she rubbed the herbs in. Rocking backwards, she turned the candle in her hands. She repeated this until some intuition told her it was enough.

She looked back at Selene for direction.

"Close your eyes again," Selene said, "and imagine things coming to light. Things being revealed. Hold the candle in your hands until you feel like you've got that idea strongly in your head and then breathe across the candle three times."

Cassie thought of the power of the moon and the sun. She thought of the power of turning on the lamp in a darkened room. She thought of secrets being revealed. Of shame, but also of desire. She thought about things hidden so far deep inside, a person wasn't even conscious of what they were.

What was she hiding? She didn't know, but had sense of it swimming beneath the waters, and she remembered the tarot card of the Moon. And all the hidden creatures coming up from the ocean depths.

"Show me the dark," she said. "I need to see the darkness." And she saw ripples on black water. And moving images.

"That's it. That's what I need," she said. "Show me the hidden faces. Let the darkness be revealed."

Cassie opened her eyes again. Selene just nodded.

"Put the candle in the holder," they said. "And when you feel ready, strike a match, and say three times. 'Let what is hidden be revealed. Let there be justice.' Hold the High John the Conqueror in your left hand, and hold your right hand out towards the candle as you speak."

Cassie picked up the root. It felt heavier than it did before. More solid somehow. It was rough under her fingers, and despite its heft, was still just the right size to fit inside her palm with her fingers curled around it.

Holding her right hand out toward the candle flame, she took in a deep breath, remembering to center herself first, and making sure her feet were flat on the ground. Solid. She made sure her breathing was slow and even. Then she drew in a great draft of air.

"All the powers of the waning moon, please heed my call. Hear my request." She sat still for a moment, looking at the flickering candle flame. Focusing on the layers of it. The clear space right at the wick. The blue just around it edging out towards orange and yellow. That flame had magic. "Let what is hidden be revealed. Let there be justice."

She licked her lips. Took another breath.

"Let what is hidden be revealed. Let there be justice," she spoke a second time. She could feel the energy in the room change. The candle flame started to flicker, flare, and hiss.

"Let what is hidden be revealed. Let there be justice!"

The candle flame flared until it was two inches long. Cassie breathed and stared. Something felt different. The walls of the room bulged in and then out again. Cassie broke out in a sweat. Selene looked like they were deep underwater. And then Cassie was in a different room, staring at a dark misty figure standing over a man who sat reading in a battered leather armchair.

What the—?

He looked at her, dark eyes startled.

And then the image was gone. She was in Selene's attic apartment, her coven mate's pale face staring at Cassie from beneath dark lashes.

The root fell from Cassiel's hand.

8

JOE

This was a tricky one, and Joe hadn't slept very well after the weird whatever-the-hell-it-was event the night before.

"You look like shit, bro," Henry said, gloved hands gripping the other end of a piece of Sheetrock they were preparing to wrestle into place next to the stairwell. "You should have just gone out drinking with me. You might look better this morning."

Joe and his brother were trying to build a wall in the attic. The space was cavernous, despite the barely eight-foot ceilings, and they wanted to make it into two separate spaces, so there was an actual bedroom up there instead of just a big, open loft. But there was no good way to build the wall without having to straddle the stairwell opening.

If they put boards across the gaping maw, it was going to interfere with the wall's placement. So Joe, being the taller of the two, and with longer legs, was the designated nail wielder.

His brother stood on the floor of the attic room itself,

holding the Sheetrock. They'd already framed the wall in. That had been the easy part. You could stand on solid floor for that. But putting up the Sheetrock? Good God, this was a pain in the ass.

Henry held one end of the Sheetrock steady, boots planted firmly on the wood floor, and Joe straddled the space as best he could, one foot on an extendable metal ladder, folded out and braced against a stair tread.

The other foot was on the far side of the opening, where a railing should be if there was one. It was neither comfortable nor particularly safe, but since they worked for themselves, they didn't have to worry too much about OSHA.

Thank God for whoever invented a nail gun, at least. It made life so much easier. Joe swung the gun up. *Snick. Snick. Snick.* The nails thunked home.

"Did you meet any women last night, bro?"

"Yeah. You know, it was pretty cool scene. You should have been there. There were actually a lot of hot women."

"Any of them interesting?"

His brother laughed. "You know me. They're *all* interesting."

"You *loove* women," Joe said.

"Yep. How about you?" his brother asked. "Have you met anyone lately?" Deliberately casual. That was his brother. Not voicing the worry directly, but worried all the same.

"I'm not telling you a thing, bro."

Snick. Snick. Joe moved the nail gun over and braced himself against the Sheetrock. His arms were getting tired of holding up his end and wielding the nail gun at the same time.

"Wait, did you actually meet somebody? Tell me about her."

Joe shook his head and smiled. "If ever met somebody, you think I'd actually tell you? You'd swoop right in with that charm of yours. It's what you always do."

Joe wasn't going to tell Henry he'd been mooning over Tarika last night. Or that a gorgeous mystery woman with red hair had shown up in the middle of it all. Some weird-ass apparition that looked just like one of Raquel's baristas.

"I do *not. Man,* you're cold. Think I'd steal my brother's woman?"

"Well, she's not my woman," Joe said. "I barely just met her. But I know how you are with a pretty face."

"I do like 'em. But seriously. Tell me about her."

Snick. Snick. Almost there.

"Her name is Cassie. She has the most amazing red hair I've ever seen. She's pretty. Quiet. She's hot. Well, I think she's hot. But I don't know if you would. She's not really your type."

"Is she your type? And you want me to come over and hold that end? Seem's like this side's secure enough for now."

"I don't have a type, you know that. And yeah. Let me sink a few more nails, then move to the landing."

"Where'd you meet her?"

"She works at Raquel's café."

"Oh, you know, I think I've seen her walking down the street. Super-long red hair?"

"Well, she had it up when I met her. You know, for working in the café. But it looks like it was probably long."

"Yeah. She's pretty. Hey, there's some music playing down at the Constellations tomorrow night. You up for that?"

"I might be," Joe said. After last night's weirdness, it'd be good to actually get out and be around people again. "What time?"

"It's early, actually. Things start around eight o'clock. Thought we could swing by the Mercado for a burrito first."

"Sounds good. Okay. I need to move over now, so I'm not going to be able to be on the ladder anymore. You're going to have to come around to the landing now."

His brother shifted position, boots thumping behind Joe on his way to the landing. "Okay. I got you, bro."

Joe inched his left foot off the ladder and leaned with his one hand flat against a Sheetrock, the other still gripping the nail gun, holding it sideways against the Sheetrock, with his weight on one side. He waited until he got the balls of both feet semi-secure on the other side of a big, gaping hole.

"Man. I hope I can do this," he said. He still had to reach over another foot to his right to get the next row of nails sunk. "Okay, here I go."

He reached his arm out. And the phone in his pocket started wailing like a siren and vibrating. "Shit!" The nail gun dropped, clattering through the ladder and bouncing down the stairs. Joe slipped, and slammed himself down onto the ladder, bashing his head on the stairwell wall.

"Ow! Shit! Shit! Shit!"

"Oh my God, Joe! You okay?"

"No." It felt as if he'd cracked his wrist or something. That was going to be just great. Couldn't work with a cracked wrist. Something was wrong. Everything hurt. It felt as if one of his own ribs was poking a hole in the middle of his back. It hurt to breathe and his wrist was on fire. His head hurt. He must have smacked his ankle on the ladder when he hit, too.

"Oh, man. Okay. Just stay where you are. I'm going to call

for help. And it looks like you have enough nails up, so I'm gonna let this go."

"Okay," Joe ground out.

"Just hold tight."

Joe tried to keep breathing, but it hurt, and his phone kept wailing in his hip pocket, vibrating against his ass.

"What the fuck?" That had never happened before. Then the phone went silent. All of a sudden Joe heard his brother calling someone. Sounded like their friend Jack.

"Don't call an ambulance," Joe said.

"I need your help. Joe fell and I have to figure out a way to move this ladder without hurting him. Can you come over? Okay. Thanks."

Henry squatted at the top of the stairs.

"Jack was home. He'll be right over."

Jack was their other next-door neighbor, who lived in the house on the other side of theirs from Raquel's. He gardened a lot and was a really sweet man. Wrote video games for a living, so he worked at home most of the time in a home office with a huge computer array.

"Hello?"

"Yep! Stairs up to the attic!" his brother called down.

"Holy shit! What happened?"

"My phone. Went crazy. And I slipped."

"How bad are you hurt?"

"I don't know. Semi-bad," Joe grated out through clenched teeth. God, everything hurt.

"Okay," Jack's voice rumbled. "What do you need, Henry?"

"I'm going to try to move Joe. Get him out of the way of the ladder. Jack, I need you to try to collapse the ladder so we can get it out of here and carry Joe down."

"Carry me?"

"I don't know how bad you're hurt, bro. Let's just get this done and find out, okay? Chill."

"Oh my God," Joe murmured.

"You ready?" Jack asked.

"I'm on the ladder still! You can't move it. I can't move!"

"Shit," Henry said. "Okay, bro. I'm gonna get under your armpits and try to shift you up the stairs some. Okay?"

Henry's boots thumped down until they were even with Joe's head. Joe hissed as his brother's hands wiggled their way under his back, toward his armpits. He felt the fingers reach toward the front, gripping his pecs.

"I'm gonna move you now."

Henry pulled and Joe screamed. He couldn't help himself. Pain shot through his whole body.

Henry didn't stop.

Joe's feet and legs clattered off the metal ladder. Joe screamed again.

"Clear!" Joe heard Jack shout.

Henry sat down with a thump.

"Fuck," Joe said, tears streaming down his face.

"Sorry, bro."

Joe heard the clattering of the ladder. He guessed Jack was trying to collapse the thing and get it out of the way.

"What now?" Jack said.

"Can you get a blanket from Joe's bed?" Henry asked. "We're going to need a sling to carry him in."

"Oh God," Joe said. "I don't want you to move me."

"I know. But we have to get you to urgent care. Maybe even the hospital. We could still call an ambulance."

Joe just lay there for a moment, stair treads digging into his back, sharp rib making every breath hurt. His left wrist and right ankle throbbed, and something was seriously messed up with his back.

He wished he could just go to sleep. Make the whole situation go away.

"So stupid. My fucking phone."

"Joe?" Henry asked again.

"No. We don't have the money for an ambulance." He sighed. "Just do your best."

9

CASSIEL

It was late afternoon and the café was closed. A light snow had started to fall outside. Cassie hoped the buses would still be running when she was done with her closing chores. You never knew with Portland buses.

Portland didn't get enough snow to warrant more than a handful of snowplows, and people didn't remember to keep chains in the trunks of their car.

Luckily, there wasn't enough snow yet for vehicles as heavy as the TriMet buses to need chains. If it started snowing any more heavily, though, Cassie might be out of luck.

She went back to filling squat glass shakers with the gold crystals of demerara sugar. The napkin dispensers were next.

Raquel was hanging art. Usually the artists would do it themselves, but Josephina used a wheelchair, which made hanging paintings above café booths pretty impossible. She and Raquel had decided it was easier for her to just have someone drop her paintings off. She said she trusted Raquel to hang them at the right height. Josephina had left Raquel notes, though, detailing which painting followed another in sequence.

The paintings were beautiful. Cassie loved the bright colors Josephina used. Rich reds and golds. Turquoise. Deep purples.

The paintings were abstracts that just gave a hint of landscape. Cassiel could tell that really they were paintings of Portland. Here was the long, curved arch of the Steel Bridge. There was Mount Hood. The fountain at Pioneer Square. Cassie couldn't figure out how Josephina did it, how she managed to make something look so abstract and so concrete at the same time.

Cassie screwed the lid back on the big sugar container and turned to refilling napkin dispensers as Raquel adjusted the paintings. Raquel had just finished pounding a nail and was making sure the two–by-three acrylic piece, this one looking like the sweep of the Columbia River, hung straight above one of the booths. She stepped back, tilting her head from side to side.

"Looks good," Cassie said. "I really like these."

"Yeah. Josephina just gets better and better. Pretty soon she'll have to start charging real money for this stuff."

She picked up another painting and held it up to the wall, then double checked the list on the booth table.

"Wrong one." Raquel flipped through the stack of paintings leaning against the booth seat and slipped one free. "How are things going with the Tenants Union?"

"Not great. I mean, they're being super helpful, but I just don't think there's much to be done. I think my landlord is just a shithead and I'm going to get kicked out."

"Do you have any money saved?"

"What do you think?" Cassie said. "Sorry. I mean, I love my job. I love working here. You're awesome, Raquel, but I don't exactly make enough to save. I barely made enough to pay the rent. And moving out here from Tennessee took every bit of savings I had. I'll get my last month's rent back, I guess. But that's not much."

Raquel shook her head and clucked. "I don't know what is wrong with people. I don't know why people decide they've got to have more than they need."

"I don't either. Hey, Raquel, can I ask you about something else?"

"Sure."

"So, something happened last night that kind of freaked me out. Selene helped me do some magic...you know, to help with my housing situation. And that all went great, I think. I hope. We'll see if it helps."

Raquel nodded as she continued to work. "You never know with magic. You always have to let it take its time."

"Right. But I feel pretty good about what happened."

"So what's the problem?" Raquel kneeled on the booth seat and held the new painting up against the wall. Marked the top edges with a pencil. Putting the pencil back in her mouth, she picked up a nail and started hammering.

"We were almost done," Cassie continued. "And all of a sudden the room, you know, Selene's apartment, it started to get weird. Like wonky. And I looked at Selene to see if they noticed anything and it was like I was looking at them from under water."

Raquel stopped pounding. She set the hammer down and turned. Her eyes grew sharp, intense, as if she was trying to see what Cassie was describing. Not just in this world but some other place.

Cassie didn't have that witch's trick yet. She wasn't trained well enough.

"And?" Raquel said.

"You know that plumber friend of yours, Joe?"

Raquel just nodded again, arms crossed over her chest.

"I...somehow ended up in his living room. I guess. I don't know. He was sitting there. In a big leather chair with a beer in his hand. He looked... I don't know how he looked. Sad. Angry. Worried. And then he looked up and saw me. And I panicked and the whole scene just popped like a bubble and I was back in Selene's apartment."

And there was a ghost leaning over him, but I'm oh-so-not-ready to tell you about that yet. Because I really hope it just goes away.

"What do you think it means?" Raquel said.

Yeah. Cassie was *so* not going to get into the discussion of whatever it was she'd seen on Solstice Eve. Or the fact that she thought Joe was being haunted.

"I have no idea. I only met the guy once, when he came to fix the sink. I have no connection with him."

"He called you to him," Raquel said.

"That's what Selene said. But, I don't see how. He doesn't know me. Why would he call me? Like, why wouldn't he call *you*? You're his friend. *You're* the powerful witch here."

Raquel shook her head and made those clucking, tsk-tsking sounds with her tongue against her teeth again. "You need to stop that right there." She raised one finger. "You need to stop saying you're not powerful. You need to stop giving that shit away. You have power, just as much as I do, or Selene, or anyone else in our coven. And until you own up to that, this bad shit is going to keep happening to you."

"Wait a minute. We were talking about Joe, and now you're saying, what? My getting kicked out is my fault? That's where we're going with this? No offense, Raquel, but that's kind of harsh."

Raquel came over and sat down across from Cassie.

"Cassiel, that's not what I meant. I'm sorry. Of course getting kicked out of your apartment isn't your fault. I blame the landlord for that one-hundred percent. Thing is, though, you're not helping yourself enough. There's more you can be doing."

Raquel paused. "Whose idea was it to do magic last night?"

"Selene's."

"Right. It took them to point out to you that doing magic was something that should even happen. Why was that?"

"I don't know. I just didn't even think of it."

"See, the thing is," Raquel said, "a witch? She *always* thinks of magic. Because a witch knows where her power lies. She knows what her skills are. She knows what her weaknesses are. She knows when to work on the earth plane. She knows when to work on the astral plane. She knows when something physical needs to happen, and when magic needs to be brought in. And usually, a problem like the problem you're having now? A witch knows she needs to work that on *every* level, Cassie. And if you *believed* in yourself, you would believe in the power of the magic to help you."

Cassie sat back, shoulders rounded forward. "I just feel... defeated. You know, like, deflated. And you all are so good at everything. I barely know anything."

"Know your worth, Cassie. Claim it. Tell me what your skills are. Right now."

"I..." Cassie froze.

"Now. Tell me."

Cassie took a breath, and let the exhalation soften the edges of her body, just like she'd been taught.

"I'm good at sensing people's feelings?" she said, voice

rising into a question mark. "I... Guess I'm getting better at tarot."

I see ghosts. And sometimes see who killed them.

"And what else?"

"I'm psychic," she said quietly.

"What was that? I didn't hear you." Raquel actually cupped a hand behind one ear. Cassie knew she was being tested.

Cassie looked at her boss, her friend, her coven mate. Her cheeks burned, she was so embarrassed. She cleared her throat.

"I'm psychic."

"That's right, you are. It's about time you owned up to it. The coven needs you. *You* need you. Seems like Joe needs you too."

"So what do I do?" Cassie asked.

"When Joe comes in through the door—and he's going to any day now, maybe any minute—you're going to talk to him. And you're going to figure out how to help him. And you're going to do whatever magic Selene told you to do. You're going to figure out how to help yourself."

"But..."

Raquel held up a finger again. "*And*, you're going to remember you have a whole coven full of people who have your back. You haven't been asking for help, and that's part of your problem too. A witch knows she can't do it alone. She never can. A witch who thinks she can go it alone? There's a witch whose power starts to twist on itself. Bad things happen. I've seen it."

Raquel pushed herself back from the table. "Don't let it happen to you."

10

JOE

J oe hobbled down the sidewalk, past sleeping winter lawns, and midday folks-at-work empty driveways, thankful it was relatively dry. Also, the light dusting of snow had all melted before things froze again so there was no ice. Otherwise he would have been in a world of trouble. No way would he have made it out of the house with ice on the ground.

The tree branches were bare and reaching toward the clouds, and the air smelled like more snow was on the way. The clouds were still that weird dark gray. Darker than the usual rain clouds.

A bus rumbled by and a jogger slogged past, all bundled up in a hat and scarf. That was dedication.

Joe was in so much pain from his wrist and ribs that he should still be in bed. But he was also stubborn. And bored. And there was a gorgeous woman with red hair who just might be working today.

But the café felt further away from home than it ever had. The usual seven-minute walk had already stretched to well beyond that, and his leg was killing him. His hips were starting to complain, too, from using the cane.

He hoped the pain wasn't a preview of how he was going to feel after he hit forty. His middle-aged friends in the trades all started complaining about their elbows, knees, and backs around that age.

Joe's cane hit a piece of gravel and jerked his hand. He winced.

That accident was so stupid, he couldn't believe it. And he still couldn't figure out what the heck had happened with his phone. The phone itself was fine. He'd looked at it after they'd gotten back from the hospital—despite his protests, they *had* dragged him to the hospital and spent three hours there—to make sure the screen hadn't cracked or anything.

At any rate, after Henry and Jack had gotten him home and up the stairs, and with a pain pill and some water inside of him, he'd scrolled through all the recent calls. There was no one. Literally not one. Another mystery that was starting to freak him out.

He didn't know what to do about it, but he did know he needed to talk to that woman, Cassiel. That was the other weird thing. That somehow she'd shown up in his living room. He didn't know what that was about. But he was determined to find out. If he could force himself to speak to her.

And finally, he turned the corner from the residential streets to the row of shops and other businesses, and there was the café, lights glowing warm through the plate glass window onto the gray day.

He walked into the little protected doorway and propped his cane against the window filled with fliers for local concerts and a sign declaring "Hate Has No Business Here" and a second that simply read "Black Lives Matter."

This was going to be a tricky move. He had to grab the doorknob with his right hand—the one that wasn't in a sling—then pick up the cane before the door closed, because he couldn't shove a foot in there to keep it open.

"I got you, man." A young man in a red plaid shirt was all of a sudden in the doorway, holding it open.

"Thanks, man." Joe picked up his cane and hobbled in.

Raquel glanced up from behind the counter.

"Oh my Goddess, Joe! What happened to you?"

Cassiel whipped her head around from where she was making sandwiches, a blue apron over an oversized, white thermal shirt and skinny black jeans. Her jaw dropped.

"Um, that looks painful," she finally said.

Joe grimaced. He really didn't like being fussed over. But if he had to get fussed over by beautiful women he guessed maybe that was okay. And at least Raquel was here to run interference with his anxiety today.

"Yeah, it was weird," he said. "Stupid work accident."

"Stupid work accident?" Raquel raised an eyebrow so high it almost touched the orange scarf tying back her dreadlocks. "In all the years I've known you, you have never had a 'stupid work accident'."

Joe could feel his skin heat up. Damn his blush reflex. He hated it. He was just glad his skin had enough color to mask it. At least he hoped so.

"I can't really explain it," he said.

"Why don't you sit down? I'll bring you a coffee," Raquel said.

"That would be great."

Cassiel just looked at him for another moment, her light gray eyes holding his. He fought to not look away. Then she turned back to finish making the sandwich she was working on.

There was a strangeness that hovered around her. She was beautiful, but there was something uncanny about her. That something reminded him a little bit of the stories his grandmother used to tell him when he was little and they would visit the islands. She had died the year Joe turned thirteen. He missed her still.

Cassiel was like some kind of fairy creature. His grandmother said they lived in the heiaus, or nature temples, in the trees. Yeah, she was a pale-skinned, redheaded wood sprite or something. A sandwich-making wood sprite.

Raquel brought his coffee over after adding some cream and half a teaspoon of sugar. She sat down across from him at the table, a bright red cup in her own hands.

"Joe," she asked softly, "what's really going on?"

He sighed, and blew across the surface of his coffee.

"I don't know, Raquel," he said. "It was the strangest thing. I was putting up a wall in our attic with Henry, and I was bracing myself, straddling the opening to the stairwell. I was just about to sink the last few nails in and be done with the job...and my phone went crazy. And I fell."

Her eyes looked as concerned as if Joe was her son Zion —named after the safe space in *The Matrix*, not the place in the Bible. Raquel was another geek. Probably why they got along.

"Oh, Joe. Who was calling you?"

"Well, that's the weird thing," he said. "No one. And it wasn't even like a phone call. It was like a siren, blaring and ringing and vibrating all at once. No one was calling me, and I can't figure it out. Things have been weird, Raquel. Like, I've been seeing things."

He looked down at his coffee cup. "I've been *feeling* things, and I don't know what to think. I don't know who to talk to about this stuff."

Joe grinned then. "I mean, you're the only witch I know, and you've been a little busy."

"Well, you actually know two witches," she said. She jerked her head back towards Cassiel.

"Cassiel's a witch? Well, that explains a lot."

"And just what do you mean by that?" Raquel said.

"I could swear I saw her the other night when I was sitting in my living room."

"Actually, she mentioned something like that to me."

Cassiel swished past them her skinny black jeans and her oversized white shirt, carrying the sandwich to a customer sitting at the window counter, trailing the scent of pine trees and loam behind her.

Joe inhaled. She smelled like a forest. Like damp earth. One of his favorite scents.

"I heard that," she said as she passed.

Joe's face flushed again.

"Oh, never mind. Cassie's cool," Raquel said.

"Great. She's going to think I'm crazy."

"And why would she care about that?" Raquel said, grinning. "Never mind. Drink your coffee."

He did. It was perfect. Smooth and rich with a slightly nutty undertone. Joe swore sometimes he loved coffee more than anything else.

"You make the best coffee, Raquel."

"I know," she said. "But what are we going to do about all this stuff that's haunting you?"

"What do you mean, haunting? You think I have a ghost?"

She just shrugged. "You sure as heck have something. A man like you doesn't just freak out and fall into a stairwell. Something's trying to get your attention."

Raquel looked over her shoulder. "Cassie?"

Cassiel was back behind the counter, stacking clean coffee cups on top of the espresso machine. "Yeah?"

"Why don't you sit with Joe for a minute? I've got some things to do."

"Okay, let me just get myself a coffee first. I'll take my break."

Great. Just what he needed. He'd actually come in here to talk to Cassiel, but now he felt uncomfortable again. Talking to Raquel was easy. She was a friend. Talking to a woman like Cassiel? Joe was starting to sweat.

What a dork.

That's what Henry would say. But Joe *was* a dork. He always had been. Aaannd, there she was, red hair piled up on her head, loose white shirt swirling around her slim hips, long sleeves shoved up her pale arms.

Cassiel set her red cup of cappuccino down on the table with a thunk, set down her phone, and sat across from him.

He blushed again. *Damn it, Joe,* he thought. *Chill out.* He could barely look at her, which he knew was bad. Weird. *Okay, get it together, Joe.*

He took a deep breath and forced himself to raise his eyes to look at her again. Her grey eyes stared calmly back, and locked with his.

Definitely a spark there. He didn't think he was imagining it.

"Are you okay?" she asked finally, breaking their gaze and looking at his sling.

"Yeah. I'll be fine. No problem. You know, you work in construction, you get hurt sometimes."

"That's not what it sounded like to me," she said.

"Oh. You heard all that."

"I have pretty good ears."

"Yeah." He looked back down at his coffee. Took another sip.

"Actually..." he said. Cassiel just waited, stirring her cappuccino with a little spoon. Lifting some foam on the spoon, she put it in her mouth.

God, just eating foam off a cappuccino, she was sexy. Shit.

"Actually?" she finally said.

"Actually, I, um, did want to talk to you. I was wondering if you might want to have dinner tonight. You know, early. When you get off work." Henry wouldn't mind if he blew him off. At least, Joe hoped not.

Cassiel looked off to the side, as if she were thinking, the overhead lights gleaming on her red hair.

"Yeah, that should work. I have a meeting I have to go to later, but I could do dinner. Where do you want to meet?"

Not an enthusiastic answer, but good enough.

"Okay, great. Great. How about Cabalen? You ever been there? Filipino food."

"Not yet. But it sounds good."

"Well, I guess you have to get back to work."

She smiled and glanced at her phone. "Not just yet. So. What's wrong with your arm?"

"Cracked my wrist—a hairline fracture—and sprained it. Doctor said I was lucky nothing shattered. It's bad enough, though. I can't work. Henry's being good about it, but I think he's a little annoyed."

"Henry?" she asked.

"That's my brother. I have my plumbing business, but we have a business together, too. Construction. Rehabbing old buildings, finish work, all that kind of stuff."

"That's so cool," she said. "I wish I had a skill like that."

Joe shrugged, wincing as it pulled on his sling. "Everyone has some kind of skill. I bet you have plenty."

"Yeah. I'm not sure yet. Maybe."

Joe had meant to talk to her today about the fact that she'd shown up in his house, but that felt too awkward. Plus, there was still something strange about her. He wasn't sure if he was one-hundred-percent comfortable. As if he'd ever be one-hundred-percent comfortable with a woman he found attractive.

"Well," Cassie said after he'd been silent for a while. She finished off her cappuccino. "Maybe I should get back to work. See you at dinner."

"Yeah. See you at dinner."

She picked up her cup. "Bye, Joe." And then turned to walk away.

"Later, Cassiel."

She turned back. "You can call me Cassie."

He smiled. "Okay, Cassie."

Joe let out a breath as she turned away again. Maybe he hadn't blown it too badly. He could never tell. Well, he guessed he would find out.

11

CASSIEL

W as it a date? Or a consultation? Cassiel wasn't sure, but she was trying to learn to go with the flow these days.

She was certainly attracted enough to Joe for this to be a date. But she still had trouble getting a read on him.

At any rate, the place smelled amazing. A combination of vinegar, sesame oil, roasted pork, and a whole bunch of spices Cassie couldn't identify. The decor was simple: pale yellow walls and square pressboard tables with black padded stacking chairs. Plants with leafy fronds crouched in every corner of the room, and what looked like some local art hung on the walls.

It turned out the Filipino restaurant was just up the street from the café. She'd never eaten there before. Joe said he and Henry went there all the time.

His skin tone still looked a little more washed out than it ought to be, likely from pain, but Cassie was reminded that Joe was a handsome guy. He wore a soft-looking navy-blue flannel shirt, open at the neck with a bright white T-shirt peeking out. She wondered how he'd gotten his injured wrist through the armhole.

She wisely decided not to ask. The guy still seemed a little skittish, eyes darting toward her, then at the table, or the menu, or anyplace other than her eyes.

"Wow. This looks so good." She perused the plastic-encased menu.

"Yeah, they do it up right. It's not Melanesian, but it's still pretty good." He smiled. The guy was actually trying to make a joke. Good for him. Maybe by the end of dinner he'd actually be relaxed enough to tell her what he wanted to talk about.

"So, what, are *you* Melanesian? And isn't that close to the Philippines?"

Joe nodded. "Just a few islands over from where my people are from."

"Do you ever get back there? I mean, were you born there? Or were you born here?"

"Oh, my brother and I were born in Portland. It's what we know. But I still have some family back on the islands. We used to get over there every few years when I was a kid. My mom lives there now. And my grandma never left. She's pretty cool. Sometimes I think she's a witch like Raquel. She talked about all kinds of magic stuff."

Cassie smothered a smile and caught Joe cheating his eyes at her again. He quickly looked back down at his menu.

"A witch like you," he mumbled.

"What was that?" Cassie asked. She'd heard him, but wanted to poke him a bit. See how he'd respond.

Joe cleared his throat. "Raquel tells me you're a witch."

Cassie set her menu down and started playing with her fork. "Yep. Been in Raquel's coven for just over a year now."

"You like it?" Joe said.

"Yeah, it's great. The people are great."

"I mean, what do you guys do? Are you allowed to talk about it?"

"Well, yeah, there's not too much that's secret. I mean, there's some stuff we're not supposed to talk about, but it's good. We get together once a month. Sometimes twice. We work together at the full moon usually, but sometimes at the dark moon. And then there's these big solar holidays. The fire feasts."

"Like what?"

"Well, it was just Winter Solstice Eve. You've heard of that, right?"

"Yeah. Longest night of the year."

"We did a big ritual." That she was still avoiding thinking about.

"Huh. That's cool. Like, do you guys like celebrate Halloween and shit? Sorry."

"That's okay," Cassiel said. "You can curse around me. Just don't curse *at* me. But yeah. Halloween's a big one. Samhain, we call it. And Beltane. That's May Day."

"You mean like the workers struggle day?"

Cassie smiled again and laughed. "Well, no, not the workers struggle day, although a few of the coven members celebrate both holidays. Speaking of workers, my meeting tonight is in the union hall down the street."

"Those guys are pretty cool," Joe said. "I work with them on jobs sometimes. Electricians union. All that jazz."

Cassie took a sip of water.

"That's the nice thing about having a family business, though. We don't need a union." He grimaced, glancing down at his sling. "Of course, it also means I don't exactly get worker's comp."

The waitress walked over, "You ready to order?"

They both placed their orders, pork for Joe, and some kind of chicken dish for Cassie.

"Can we get some tea, Rosamie? Thanks."

After the waitress walked away, Joe actually looked at Cassie.

"How long do you have to wear that?" Cassiel asked.

"I don't know," he said. "Doctor said I shouldn't really use my wrist for a few weeks."

"Oh man, Joe. Does that totally mess you up?"

"Pretty much," he said. "But this time of year, sure we have some jobs, but they're the smaller ones. All interiors. People save their big outdoor projects for the spring and summer here, you know."

"Right. Rain and snow," Cassie said.

"Portland? Mostly rain," Joe said. "We get used to working in all weather, though. If you waited for the rain to stop. we'd never get any work done. And in winter, I get to deal with burst pipes. Gonna have to shunt those calls off, I guess."

Cassie was rapidly deciding that she liked him. She liked that he was a little awkward. She really liked his big dark eyes. But there was also something wrong about him. Something off. It was as if there was a dark cloud around his aura.

And that something was picking at him. Chipping away at his edges, making him less firm and strong. A man like Joe? She bet under ordinary circumstances he was solid. Something was definitely wrong.

She reached out and touched his arm. It zapped her, as if there were an electrical shock.

"What the—?" Joe said.

"Sorry. I don't know what happened. That was weird. I just felt like I needed to touch you, like... I don't know why it sparked like that, though."

Unless her attraction was generating actual electricity all of a sudden, which was a stupid thought.

Cassie ran her hands over her hair, then shook out her fingers. Then she realized something. How stupid. Of course. The woman's message, on Solstice Eve.

"Wait. *You're* Joe," she blurted out, as the waitress set down their tea. The waitress gave her a strange look, then looked at Joe, shrugged, and walked off again.

"Uh. Yeah. I thought you knew that."

Right. He was really going to think she was a freak. Oh well. She didn't need to start dating now anyway, did she?

"No. That's not what I mean. This is a little awkward. I mean we just met recently and all, but there's something going on…I think there's something wrong with you."

"With *me*? Thanks a lot," he said. "That makes a guy feel good."

He looked a little offended. She couldn't blame him.

"I'll…yeah, well. Not like that. I just…" Cassie leaned toward him. "So I'm a little bit psychic."

Joe just sat there. Looking at her. Then he must have realized he was staring, and looked away.

"What's that mean?" he said.

"It means I can sense things sometimes. And sometimes *see* things. Like things that most people don't even know are there."

She felt him get very still across the table from her.

"Do you think you can find out what's bugging me? Because I've been feeling something too. Like the other night, I was sitting in my living room and I could have sworn someone was watching me. But there was no one there. I even got up and closed the curtains. It felt like there was someone in the room. And then my phone going crazy… I don't know what that was about either."

Cassie just waited. She wondered if she should say anything, or wait for him to mention it.

"I saw you that night," she finally said.

Joe looked up, eyes haunted. "I saw you too. What was *that* about?"

She shook her head. "I don't know. All of a sudden I was just pulled to you, and I saw you sitting there. But then the whole thing popped like a soap bubble. I couldn't see you anymore. Did you call me?"

"I don't think so," Joe replied. He looked really uncomfortable. "But. But I don't know. I mean. I don't know anything anymore. You know, I used to just be this steady guy. Straight ahead. Just rode my skateboard. Worked with my brother. Had a couple beers. You know. Easy. And then... And then my girlfriend dies."

"Oh, Joe." Cassie could tell this was really hard for him to say.

"Yeah. Tarika died and, you know, I was mourning for a while, but then I thought things were getting better. I thought I was coming out of it and feeling pretty good. And then things started to get weird."

It was Cassie's turn to get still and quiet inside. This shouldn't be happening. She looked at this man so obviously in pain and the witch in her wanted to help him. But she also wanted to run as far away as she could.

That woman appearing to her during the Solstice ritual. And now Joe's girlfriend. Was that who had been leaning over his chair?

No.

They couldn't be ghosts. She really thought she'd blocked that part off. Hadn't let herself see a ghost in two years. Not since she left Tennessee, and the blood, and the anguish, and the police lights flashing, and the struggle to prove in the real world what the ghosts were telling her from beyond.

Cassie started shaking her head.

"Cassie?"

The waitress was back with the food. Cassie wasn't sure she felt like eating anymore, but she had to act normal. As if all this were okay.

The smell of the food made her want to vomit. Damn it. She tried to slow her breathing down, get some air deep inside her belly. It wasn't working.

"You okay?" he asked. "You're not looking so good."

Clammy sweat started beading up on her forehead.

"I don't feel so great all of a sudden. I don't think I can eat..."

She looked into his brown eyes, so filled with concern. She couldn't...

"I'm sorry, Joe. I think I have to go."

Cassie shoved her chair back and gathered up her coat and messenger bag. She needed to get away from him. Now.

Joe rose. "Do you want to take some food, at least?"

"No. No. I'm sorry. I just have to go."

"Cassie, wait..."

12

JOE

Constellations was jammed.

Every tiny table in the front area near the bar was occupied, and the scarred sweep of the bar itself was three deep with people trying to get drinks. The open floor around the pocket-sized stage was full of talking, laughing clumps of friends.

The place smelled of spilled beer and that old marijuana scent that always got trapped in the clothing of regular smokers. Whiskey. Mingled perfumes and colognes. Freshly washed hair. A little bit of body odor from folks coming off work.

And even on a Tuesday night, there was an air of fun. Anticipation. Expectation. People must really like the band that was about to come on. Joe didn't remember the band's name, but it turned out Henry knew the bass player.

It was nice to feel people so happy. *People need some happiness*, Joe thought. Hell, *he* needed some happiness. He toyed with his phone, staring at the wallpaper of a turned newel post from his favorite building, trying to figure things out. How did a person even think about a call that didn't appear on his phone?

The weird alarm-going-off-not-a-call that had led to an arm in a sling and a temporary cane.

His phone offered up no explanation. Just like it did the last five times he'd checked it.

Constellations was probably the last place a person with an injured leg and wrist should be. It was too damn crowded.

Joe didn't like crowds. Henry, though? Henry was in his element.

"Bro!" His brother clapped his shoulder on the uninjured side. "Do you need another beer?"

"No, I'm good thanks."

Henry lit up in a crowd. Must be an extrovert. Joe liked things a little quieter. A little simpler. Sure, he loved hanging out with friends. He even liked hearing music. But maybe he just wasn't in the mood that night.

At first, Henry had found him a little table to sit at, thinking he could put his foot up, but Joe had nixed the idea. The table was too much in the middle of things and Joe was terrified someone was going to bump into him. The last thing he needed was to get re-injured and be out of work for longer. Henry quickly found him a spot at the bar, likely offering to buy someone's drink to give up their spot, so here he was, leaning up against the side wall, propped up on a stool, trying to keep out of people's way. The bar was a better place to observe from, anyway.

He took a sip from his pint glass, a local IPA. Pretty good. A little citrusy.

"Hey man, what happened to you?"

Joe looked up. Okay. This was going to get interesting.

It was Darius. His big, handsome head stared down at Joe. Close-cropped hair; gold, untucked button-down shirt over his jeans. The scent of classic Polo Blue. He was one gorgeous man, and Joe could see the resemblance to Tarika.

He had to admit that hurt.

"Darius! Hey."

"This seat taken?"

"All yours, man."

Darius pulled out the stool next to Joe and sat down. "Can I get a Jameson's, rocks?" he asked the bartender, a woman in her forties with green hair that didn't quite match her green eyes.

"Sure thing," she said.

He turned to Joe. "Can I get you anything, man?"

"No, I'm good, thanks."

"So, what happened, man?"

"Work accident. Stupid. I fell into a stairwell."

"Ouch. Damn, you hurt bad?"

"Hairline fracture and wrist sprain. Knocked up my ankle. Bruised a couple of ribs. Not too bad. Could've been a lot worse considering I fell on a ladder and stairs."

"Oh, *man*, that's terrible."

The waitress set Darius's whiskey on the bar in front of him. He smiled at her and threw some money on the bar.

"So, how you been?"

Okay, this was getting really weird. The last time Joe had seen Darius, Darius had been drunk and swinging for his head.

Henry and Jack had barely gotten Joe out of Darius's way before a couple of Darius's friends wrapped their arms around him and pulled him off.

"I'm okay," he said. "You know how it is. But I'm not sure

why you're sitting here talking to me, Darius, considering last time I saw you tried to rip my head from my shoulders."

"Man." Darius shook his head and took a sip of whiskey, rattling the big ice cube around the glass. "Yeah. That's why I'm here. I saw you across the room, and I felt bad, man. I said to myself 'I have to go apologize to that brother'."

Darius turned and looked Joe in the face. "I'm sorry, man. It just...it was the grief. I know you loved my sister. I know you had nothing to do with her death. I just... It was all so *strange*. Tarika had it going *on*. She had everything. You remember, right? She was so full of fire and passion. I still don't get how it happened."

Joe took a sip from his pint, fingers slipping a little on the condensation.

"I don't get it either. Suicide never made any sense to me."

"So. Do you think she didn't do it?" Darius asked, voice dropping.

Joe shrugged, then winced. He had to remember that shrugging pulled on his wrist. "I don't know, man. I'm starting to question everything. I'm starting to wonder..."

"Wonder what?"

"I don't know. All I know is, you're right, it doesn't make any sense. And I miss the hell out of her."

Darius took a swallow of whiskey. "Yeah, man. I miss her too."

The sound of drumsticks marking out the time snapped against Joe's ears and the band started up with a clash of chords from the electric guitar.

The bass rumbled in. And then a man's voice started spitting some rapid-fire lyrics into the microphone.

Darius leaned closer to Joe. Joe adjusted himself so he could lean in, too, without putting pressure on his injured wrist. His ankle throbbed from being on the barstool too long, but he couldn't leave now, not with Darius here.

Besides, he'd never make it through the crowd at this point. Not on his own.

Darius was pulling something out of his wallet. A news clipping. He carefully unfolded it and slid it across the bar toward Joe.

"Check this out, man."

The clipping was from the *Portland Herald*. It was about a building development in the middle stages of construction, a lot of money behind it, backing from the city, pretty much everything going for it.

The complex of apartments above—with ten percent of the units set aside for low income housing—and shops below was the classic design of recent decades of "urban living" construction. Those buildings didn't have the character of the ones Henry and Joe got contracted to refurbish, but Joe didn't mind them.

He wasn't a purist. He also had enough sense to know that housing was needed and there weren't enough gorgeous old homes to go around.

Joe tried to tune out the band so he could focus on whatever the hell it was that Darius wanted him to look for. The combo was actually pretty decent. No wonder the bar was packed on a Tuesday night. He wouldn't mind actually listening to them sometimes.

Right now, though, they were a minor annoyance.

As he scanned the piece, he still wasn't getting it.

"So, this condo complex caught fire. It happens. What are you trying to show me?"

Darius didn't say anything. He just slid a second news article across the bar. This one had clearly been printed off the internet. It was from the *Columbia Valley News*.

Another development had caught fire, this one up in Renton, near Seattle.

Joe couldn't pinpoint what was wrong, but the fingers on his non-injured side tapped on the paper, the way he did when information was very close to the surface, but not quite coming through. It was as though his body wanted to jostle the information to the surface. Jar something loose.

He picked up his pint and took a sip, then turned to Darius.

The man had his right hand wrapped around the whiskey glass, but he wasn't drinking. His eyes looked serious, with the heat of coals behind them.

"What are you after here, Darius?"

"I think Tarika was chasing a story," he said, voice low. "I think there've been a lot of these accidental fires in the Pacific Northwest, and I think Tarika was trying to find the connections."

Joe leaned back against the wall. The bar had grown warm and he was starting to sweat under his thermal T-shirt and flannel. The air was too thick. Darius, and everybody else, were too close.

"You always carry this in your wallet?" Joe gestured at the papers.

"I look at them every single day," Darius replied. "When I saw you, I knew I had to show you."

"Who else have you talked to about this?"

"No one. You're the first."

Joe sipped his beer, not sure what to say.

"You're not a reporter, Darius. You're not an investigator. What exactly are you doing with this information, man?"

Darius gave a slight shake of his head. "Nothin'. Just wondering so far. Trying to figure out why Tarika had to die. Wondering if this story had anything to do with it."

"How do you know she was working on this story? She never talked when she was onto something big."

Darius leaned closer again. Joe had nowhere to go, already jammed up against the wall. He fought to school his face and calm himself down. No need to have a panic attack in front of Tarika's brother.

"That's just it, man. After she died, I remembered that I'd mentioned that first building burning, and had some questions about it. Figured I'd ask her, since she knew everything there was to know about city hall. She didn't say much. Barely seemed interested. Just said it was too bad the extra housing was gone. And that it seemed like folks were always needing to start over in this town."

"Because she wouldn't talk about what she was working on."

"You got it, man. That's when I started searching for construction fires."

"How many do you have?"

"Too many," Darius said. "If you're in, I'll show you."

"Give me a day to process this, will you, man?"

"Take the time you need," Darius finished his whiskey, smacked the glass on the bar top, and put one warm hand on Joe's arm.

"You've got my number, man." He looked at the sling, and the cane tucked against the wall. "Take care of yourself."

"See you around."

13

CASSIEL

Cassie had walked around the block a few times, lug-soled boots keeping her feet on the sidewalk, trying to calm herself down. Trying to get herself together enough to go to this Tenants Union meeting she'd promised herself she would attend.

She hoped Joe hadn't noticed she never answered his question about the *"You're Joe"* she'd blurted out before she freaked at dinner.

Cars shushed by, likely heading home from work. People periodically joined her on the sidewalk, going to one of the few restaurants in the neighborhood, or to one of the several bars.

She still felt queasy, and searched her pockets as she walked, hoping for a ginger candy or even a breath mint. Anything to settle her roiling stomach.

What were the odds? She'd moved half a continent away, met a cute guy at work, and the guy ended up haunted.

"Damn ghosts, you just won't give up, will you?"

She had given up on them. Given up on her psychic powers. All the Gifts she envied in the rest of her coven?

Well, she had a Gift, too. She'd just held it in abeyance. Shoved it in a box.

And then shoved that box as far back into the closet of her mind as it would go.

Well, the ghosts were knocking on that closet door now and Cassiel was going to need to decide whether or not to open it.

The union hall was just ahead, a beautiful brick building with a wedge of park in front. She went to the back entrance, through a little parking lot, and eased past a couple of smokers, their cigarette tips glowing under the building overhang.

Pulling open the door, she stepped inside.

Cassie looked around, kind of bewildered, she'd never been in the union hall before and wasn't sure exactly where to go. Following the sounds of people talking led her down a hallway lined with corkboards, posters, and notices of workers' rights information, rallies, and union updates.

Yep, the meeting must be through that open door.

She walked in, was immediately assaulted by sound, bright fluorescent lighting, and the clashing scents of too many people in one place.

Cassiel had to laugh. She really hadn't expected to see a packed house. Who knew this many people were interested in local politics? Though if they were all in her position... She'd never been interested in local politics either and here she was. People crowded into stackable chairs facing away from her. A few clumps talked near the back of the room.

It looked like a cross-section of Portland, although really she realized it wasn't a cross-section, because although there were a lot of white faces as usual, there were more black and brown faces than she'd ever seen in one place in this city.

Cassie shook her head—girl, you have a lot to learn. She

never thought about it much, how white Portland was, until
something like this made her realize it.

Some children were in the back of the hall on the
ground with homework or crayons—that was what life must
be like when you were working class or poor with kids. The
kids just came with you if there wasn't a grandparent at
home or you couldn't afford a babysitter. Cassie couldn't
imagine being about to lose her home and raising children
at the same time.

All of a sudden, her situation didn't seem so bad. She
still felt pretty despondent, though. She just wasn't sure
what she was going to do. Seeing other people in the same
position didn't make it any better. They were all screwed.
How did the world end up this way, anyway?

Scanning the room, she didn't see any empty chairs, so
she found a spot on the far wall to lean against and waited.

"Okay everybody." A Latinx man in a ball cap and a light
blue work shirt stood up in front of the crowd. "Let's get this
meeting started. I'm Javier from the Tenants Union and
beside me is Olivia." A white woman with short, spiky black
hair waved her hand. Huh. It was that customer from
Raquel's. Small world.

"We're here to help you, at least we hope so. You all
know we're in a crisis here; that's why you're here. I assume
you're the people who are feeling the crisis the worst." Javier
looked around the room. "I know a lot of you have been to
our other meetings or you've come in for one-on-one help,
and I also know for a lot of you, nothing's working."

Ah shit, that wasn't what she wanted to hear. Cassie had
actually hoped there was going to be some information that
would help her. She heard other people grumbling and
groaning at that.

Javier held up his hands, "Just wait a minute, here. I

want to talk to you about something the Tenants Union has been working on. We want to pressure the city council and the mayor to force the landlords to not do no-fault evictions anymore. We want to force them to give people at least a year of transition time. And if they can't do that, we want them to give you money to move."

"If they give us money to move, where we're going to move to, bro?" another Latino man on the opposite side of the room from Cassie spoke up.

Javier nodded. "We know this isn't perfect, it's just another step along the way. The main thing is, though, we have to keep organizing."

"And how are we supposed to do that?" It was a young black woman, holding a baby on her lap. "We all work two jobs, raise our kids. All we're trying to do is keep a roof over our heads and food on the table. It's hard enough getting to these meetings; how are we supposed to do more?" The woman continued, "I know this isn't your fault; I'm not blaming you; I know you all are righteous and you do the best you can, but seriously, something's got to give. We can't go on this way."

Cassie felt angry all of a sudden. For the first time she was pissed off, because that woman was right.

Cassie had been too wrapped up in her own life. Too busy trying to help the ghosts, or not help the ghosts, trying to please people, or get people off her back. But she never thought about the larger picture until now. She wondered, could she help these people? Could she actually help herself?

"I don't know," she murmured.

"What don't you know, sister?" said a contralto woman's voice, coming from just beside her. Funny, Cassiel hadn't noticed anyone there. She spoke without looking.

"I don't know how I can help," Cassie said quietly.

"You'll be able to. We trust in you." The woman squeezed her shoulder, and Cassiel turned to look at her. She was full figured, with strong shoulders and intelligent eyes.

She was the woman from her Solstice vision.

"What the—?" And then the woman was gone.

She was a ghost. Most definitely a ghost.

Shit. Cassie's heart pounded in her chest. That had never happened to her before. She didn't just see random ghosts like that. They only came to her in distress. This woman didn't seem distressed. She seemed...capable.

"Great. Now I have *two* ghosts." Joe's ghost and whoever this woman was who decided Cassie needed to help the Tenants Union.

The squeaking of people shifting in their chairs, the talking, the coughing, the hum of the lights, all came back to Cassie.

"We need volunteers," what's-his-name was saying. Javier.

In for a damn penny... Cassie's hand shot in the air.

"Yes, you against the wall with the red hair?"

"What kind of help, what kind of volunteers?"

The white woman, Olivia, stepped forward to answer. "There are a variety of things we need help with. Staffing shifts for the tenant's hotline, knocking on doors, lobbying politicians locally or at the state capitol..."

Cassie only half listened as Olivia and Javier talked about all the help they needed. None of it pinged her inner senses as *right*. None of it felt like something a ghost would entrust her to do.

What could *Cassie* do? It had to relate somehow to her past. To the ghosts, and hunting for suspects, and all the ways she tried—and all too often failed—to lay their shades to rest.

The timing couldn't be a coincidence, two ghosts showing up within a week of one another. But what was the connection? And what did they want from her?

14

JOE

Henry would kill him for not asking for a ride, but Joe had needed to clear his head. He needed the cold winter air on his face.

It was dumb, though. He muffled a curse as his ankle screamed in pain. His fractured wrist was throbbing again and, frankly, his other wrist, his right wrist, his *good* wrist, was complaining from all the pressure the weight of his body was putting on that joint. He wasn't used to walking with a cane. He was taking it slow, still not trusting the sidewalks, even though there wasn't ice. It had rained again when he was in the bar, so things were a little slippery.

He'd had only two beers but had forgotten he'd taken a painkiller. That wasn't so smart. He was less steady on his feet than he should have been. Two pints wouldn't bother Joe on a regular night, but after a painkiller, in pain, and after *that* conversation? Yeah, Joe had been steadier than he was now.

Darius...man, he couldn't believe that guy had been holding on to this for all that time. What a thing to suspect.

Joe had heard about dirty landlords, sure. He'd even heard sketchy stories about one of the development companies in Darius's articles. When you were in the building trades in this city, you heard rumblings from every part of the business.

But the strange thing was, even though he now remembered Tarika mentioning it, she hadn't really talked about it. Which was stupid—now that he thought about it. Darius was right. Of *course* that meant she was working on something. To not talk about something as important to local politics as a big real estate development company and a possible corruption scandal?

"Shit," he said. What an idiot he'd been.

He didn't know what he was going to do with these shards of information, but he felt like Darius had entrusted him with it all, as if he was expecting Joe to do something with it.

"We got to help my sister, man," Darius had said.

"How? How are we supposed to do that?"

Darius had just looked at him with hurt eyes, as if he were a kid and Joe had just told him they couldn't have Christmas.

"Damn. Ouch." Yep, he had to get off his feet. The cold was really getting into his joints.

His phone started the siren thing again, blaring out into the night, vibrating in his pocket. Joe stumbled, caught himself with the cane.

"Shit, shit, shit." God, that hurt. "Shut up," he said.

He fumbled, shoving his cane under the elbow of his wounded arm and tried to steady himself on the slick sidewalk. He scrambled in his front pocket for his phone, and pressed the button that would shut it the hell up. He looked at the screen.

Nothing again. Just the picture of the newel post glinting up at him, lit up in the night.

"Who are you?" he asked the screen, "What do you want?"

The phone went crazy again, whooping, shaking. He pushed the button again, hard. His breath was coming faster. He was legit scared. *This shit's for real, man.*

Then he wondered if that was why Cassiel had freaked out the other night.

And then the phone rang, like just a regular, old-timey ring. He answered. "Hello? Hello?"

There was nothing, just dead air. He ended the call and looked at his phone and there was a number—*Tarika*, it said. Tarika had called him.

Joe burst into tears, sobbing on that cold sidewalk, hunched over his phone. He started to sway and, realizing he was about to fall, shoved his phone in his coat pocket and grabbed his cane again.

"Tarika, Tarika, what's happening, what do you want? I don't know how I can help you!"

A porch light went on. A cold wind rattled the bare branches of the trees above his head. He could hear the phone and electrical wires vibrating and humming.

He needed to be home. Needed a big glass of water to wash the taste of beer out of his mouth. Needed to not stink of the sweat of his effort to even stand on the sidewalk in front of sleeping houses on a freezing-cold night.

He needed to curl up in a ball and cry out his anger and frustration.

Joe wanted Cassiel. Wanted to lay his head on her lap and feel her long fingers on his temples, soothing him. Then the sharp pain of regret stabbed his chest. He wanted comfort from a woman he barely knew, when his dead girl-friend was desperately trying to call him.

It was all bullshit. Every bit of it. Joe was losing it. And it felt as if every part of him was in pain. He didn't even know how he would make it the two blocks home.

"Dammit!"

"Joe? Why the hell didn't you ask me for a ride home?" Henry had found him. Joe didn't know whether to curse or thank the universe for that.

He looked up, startled, knowing he looked a mess, tears running down his face, snot probably dripping from his nose. Great. He'd thought his brother would stay at Constellations for another hour at least. He hadn't had the energy to fight through the crowd to get to his brother, so he'd just left.

"Yeah, I'm fine, man. Just got some bad news."

"You're standing on a freezing sidewalk when you aren't in any shape to walk home. And you're cursing, which you never do."

Henry put an arm around his back, steadying him. "And you look like shit, man. Let me get you propped up against this fence here, and I'll jog home and get my truck. Give you a lift home."

Joe paused for a moment, thinking. There was no way he was going to get himself home. But he didn't want to stand out in the cold anymore.

"I just wanna get home, man. Can you help me?"

"Of course, bro."

Henry took his cane, and put an arm around Joe's waist, pulling him tight against his side.

"Let's take it slow, man. It's just two more blocks."

Joe hissed in pain. The sudden inhalation of cold, sharp air almost caused him to start coughing again. He suppressed it.

"What did Darius want?" Henry asked as they made their way down the dark sidewalk, past dark homes, a few with porch lights out front, and one or two with the flickering blue of folks binge watching television late into the night.

Joe was happy for the distraction of something other than his phone.

"Of all things, he wanted to apologize."

"Oh yeah?"

"Yeah. He said he doesn't believe I had anything to do with Tarika's death. He wanted to talk about some other stuff, too, but frankly I'm too drunk on painkillers and beer to go into it tonight."

Joe hated feeling this way. Hated feeling weak and out of sorts. He was glad Henry—who gave him shit about every other thing—would never give him shit about needing help.

Joe's foot hit a pinecone. "Damn it!"

"It's okay, bro. One more block. Let's get you across the street."

Henry helped him off the sidewalk and into the street. Cat's eyes flashed from behind a car, illuminated by the lone streetlight. Portland streets were dark at night.

Joe waited until they crossed to continue.

"All I know is Darius is suspicious about Tarika's death."

"What? That doesn't even make any sense, bro."

"I know. He was kind of talking crazy. But I didn't know what to tell him; like, he wants my help."

"Want your help with what?"

"I have no clue. He said he wants to talk to me again, but not at a bar."

"Huh. You gonna go?"

They were almost at their house, the big maple tree out front reaching its massive bare arms skyward.

Joe's phone rang again. "No. Please. Just stop."

Henry stopped him on the street and reached a hand in Joe's coat pocket.

"Hello? It's Henry on Joe's phone. Hello?" Henry ended the call.

"No one was there."

"Look at the number, man."

Henry looked from the glowing screen back up to Joe's face.

"Tarika? What the hell, man? What's going on? Is that why you were a mess back there? Did she call you?"

"Yeah." Joe nodded. "I don't know what's going on, but it's starting to freak me out. Think I'm gonna need your help, Henry. But right now, I really need to lie down."

15

CASSIEL

She couldn't believe it was happening again.

Damn it. There was no way around it: the ghosts were appearing. She thought she'd be able to avoid it. She thought she'd squashed it down—but no.

First Joe—the first man she'd been attracted to since she'd left Tennessee—walked into her work and needed something, and she had to admit it now, he was definitely being haunted.

And next, she was at a damn Tenants Union meeting, just trying to solve her own problems, and who showed up next to her? A ghost. A ghost who seemed to expect something from her. Not only that, a ghost who had already contacted her during the Solstice ritual, and also seemed to have other people behind her expecting things of Cassiel.

"We believe in you," the ghost had said. *"We trust you."*

What in all the nine worlds did that mean?

"Argh, I can't believe it!" Cassie said, stomping up the outside stairs to her attic apartment. There was a notice, fluttering on the door, with big red letters on top.

NOTICE OF RENTAL INCREASE, it said, with three crisp paragraphs beneath it, ending with a scrawled signature.

Cassiel ripped the notice from the door. Her keys jingling, she shot open the deadbolt, then the door lock, and walked into the space that had been her refuge and her home for the last two years, since she'd fled Tennessee trying to get ahead of the ghosts.

Legend had it that if you crossed water, ghosts couldn't find you anymore. Well, the thing that those legends failed to convey was that there were ghosts everywhere—north, south, east, west—no matter how many rivers or oceans a person ran over.

Her life was supposed to have gotten better. Instead, she was facing eviction brought on by an outrageous rent increase, and the ghosts were almost literally knocking down her door.

Cassie dropped her keys on the little wooden side table just inside the door, kicked off her shoes, and took the rubber bands out of her hair, letting the long fall of red cascade down her back. Her fingers scrubbed at her scalp.

"Man, I need some tea," she said.

What she *wanted* was enough alcohol to send the ghosts and her landlord on their way again, but she'd tried that years ago. It didn't last for long and it didn't really work. Well, it worked in that it blotted out her ability to see the ghosts. But it didn't make her feel any better; as a matter of fact, it made her feel sick, and it blunted all of her other psychic senses, leaving her feeling shut off from the rest of the world.

It was a horrible sickening feeling. She hated it. So Cassiel hardly drank at all anymore.

And even the Tenants Union didn't seem able to help

her landlord problems, so alcohol wasn't going to cut it, either.

Huh, she thought, as she padded to her tiny kitchen. Just a microwave, plug-in kettle, and a hotplate sitting on a counter above some cabinets.

Alcohol or not, what was she going to do about this re-emergence of ghosts? She couldn't even think about her housing issues right now.

Cassie filled the kettle at the little sink in the pocket kitchen, plugged it in, and rummaged through one of the cabinet drawers for some tea—bagged peppermint would have to do, because she didn't have Selene's store of fancy herbs. That wasn't Cassie's way, wasn't her talent.

Funny, she had started to wonder what her talent was and if she had any, and the universe was conspiring to remind her that the thing Cassie did best was talk to ghosts.

She flopped down onto the little red loveseat that sat at the foot of the bed, demarcating her living area from her bedroom, and put her stocking feet up on the coffee table. Staring at the bookshelves crammed with novels, history, and mythology, and the few pieces of bright art on the walls, Cassie didn't really see any of it.

Her eyes flickered to the altar in between two book-shelves. She should go there. She should light some candles, make some offerings, ask for help of the spirits, the ancestors.

"Forget the ancestors," she said out loud. The ghosts were ancestors—somebody's ancestors—and they all wanted too much from her.

The kettle clicked itself off.

"Pfffff," she exhaled, and got back up to make her tea. Carrying it back to the couch, she let the scent of mint wreathe around her head, inhaling deeply, hoping it would help calm her down.

She really had been about to puke in the restaurant—she probably freaked Joe out. Great. Just the way she freaked people out when she was a kid and all through high school. She'd had such a great time there—the witch, the ghost talker, the spooky bitch—everyone avoided her except for a couple of Goth kids. They were nice enough, but she didn't really have anything in common with them except they loved the fact that she saw ghosts.

They kept trying to get her to hang out at the big cemetery. As if.

Then came the too-many phone calls from the police asking for help on the down low. Down low or not, word always got out that there was another case, and that girl with the weird angel name was in the thick of it.

Cassie breathed in the mint again, then blew across the surface of the green-tinged water before setting it down on the coffee table to cool. She needed help, all right. She didn't know who to turn to; she hadn't even told her coven. They were going to be pissed.

And then there it was, tucked under the edge of her altar —a purple velvet bag, rectangular, the silvery embroidery of a full moon on the front—a tarot deck. Cassie had been trying to teach herself tarot, but she still wasn't that good at it; at least, she didn't think so. But when the cards called, she had been learning to listen.

That was one of the first things Brenda, her mentor from the coven, had taught her—"*When you're trying to train your psychic senses,*" she said, "*you have to pay attention. And if your intuition tells you to do something, or asks for something, the more you follow it, and the more quickly you follow it, then the stronger your psychic senses will become and the more your accu-*

racy will increase. You have to learn to trust yourself, Cassiel; that's the only way."

And Raquel had said almost the exact same thing. The witches were all in league with one another.

"All right, here goes," she said, and got back up off the loveseat. She brought the cards back, undid the drawstring, and slid the cool, waxed paper out onto her hands. The cards were just a little too big for regular shuffling. Breathing across the deck, she tried to center herself, tried to slow her panicked breathing down. Cassie closed her eyes and sat with the cards in her hands for a moment.

"Help me," she said. "What do I need to do about these ghosts? What's happening? Show me, please?"

She took three more long, deep breaths and then started to shuffle the cards, interleaving them hand to hand, not a poker shuffle, but a sideways shuffle. The cards slid past each other, slipping and hissing, with an occasional crack as one of them had trouble breaking through the pile. She shuffled until her hands grew still again, and she set her cards on the low coffee table next to the steaming tea, and cut the deck three times with her left hand.

"Which pile?" she asked. The middle one seemed to be glowing in her mind's eye, so she put that stack on top and then laid out three cards, left to right. The Moon, the Tower, and Death—"Uh...thanks; that's helpful."

She sat back, placed the rest of the deck on the table, picked up her tea, and sipped at the mint, letting it warm her, rolling the taste around in her mouth as she contemplated the cards.

"Well, Death, that's pretty obvious," she said to the empty room. The small refrigerator hummed in reply. "In this case, I don't think it just means change; I think it means someone's dead. Okay, ghosts—you have a sense of humor.

The Moon, bringing hidden things to light. Creatures crawling up. We got that with Selene the other night—and the Tower again, a building on fire, struck by righteous lightning, figures falling through the sky into tongues that look like flame but really are the Hebrew letter representing God."

Cassiel dragged that information from the back of her brain, from the books she'd been studying, trying to memorize what other people had said about the cards along with relying on her own intuition.

"So, maybe someone's pissed off. Maybe there's an *actual* building burning, though that's unlikely. We have the Moon —what is hidden—book-ended by two different kinds of change, Death and the Tower. The Tower shakes things up, shakes up the status quo, means an earthquake is coming." She sipped at more tea. "Or has the earthquake already come? If that's the case, what's the fallout?"

That last interpretation made the most sense to her somehow.

She felt a tapping at the base of her skull, that always happened when something was asking her to pay attention.

"Show me; tell me; what do you want me to know?" She softened her eyes and focused on her breath and looked at the Tower card again. Her eyes were focused on the flames shooting from the top of the tower.

"Fire," she said. "Change that comes from fire."

16

JOE

Joe woke to the slight, familiar pressure on his bladder and the delicious aching of morning wood.

He had a mild headache from lack of sleep and beer mixed with painkillers, but all in all, not too bad.

The air was frigid on his face, but the nest under his blankets was warm. He was in no damn hurry to get to paperwork today, that was for sure, though he told Henry he'd help him at Home Depot later.

And he should likely call his own side clients, and let them know their minor plumbing jobs were on hold for a while. Luckily, nothing on his current roster was an emergency.

He stretched out his arms.

"Shit!" he shouted, scrambling awake. "Damn, damn, damn, damn."

His right hand cradling the left, supporting it, Joe rocked himself onto this side, whimpering. He was glad he was alone. No one needed to see the pitiful wreck he was right now.

The dream had been so nice, too. It was Cassiel, red hair

flowing around her creamy white shoulders, face tipped down over his, gray eyes hazy with desire. She had just been leaning toward him, lips slightly parted, as though they'd been about to kiss.

If he wasn't still in so much pain, the morning wood he'd woken with would have still been hard and true. And he would have done something about it.

Which made Joe feel a little strange.

As if he was betraying Tarika again. She would have laughed at that, saying a little fantasy never hurt anyone. And while she was alive, that would have been true. Joe could have jacked off in the morning and made love to Tarika later that night. There would have been no doubt that his heart belonged to her, even if his mind and body sometimes desired other people, too.

Joe had never tripped about this kind of stuff before. Not the way he did now.

The light in the room was gray. After Henry had wrangled Joe up the stairs to bed, Joe had crashed immediately, only to wake up two hours later, unable to sleep.

So he'd started looking up some of those fires Darius had been talking about. He didn't get too far before sleep took him over again. But he'd seen enough to start to ask some of the same questions Darius had.

Joe sighed. He needed to clear his head. Too much beer, too many nights in a row. Joe wasn't usually a daily drinker, but the closer it got to the holidays, the easier it was to slide into a beer.

His father had died right after Christmas, four years ago, and his mother had gone to live in Fiji. Henry and Joe had argued with her, tried to talk her out of it.

"You're going to be alone," they had said. *"We'll worry about you."*

Their mother, her beautiful soft face made hard with grief, had looked at them with sad dark eyes and said, *"You'll worry if I'm here, too. And other than you two, I'll be alone no matter where I live. I may as well live someplace warm."*

That had hurt a bit, but Joe couldn't blame her. As far as he was concerned, their mother deserved any bit of ease or happiness she could get. So off she went, to stay with cousins at first, though she now had a small place of her own.

Joe kept meaning to get down there, but things never came together. He hadn't seen his mother in two years.

He rolled over onto his back again.

"I really should get up," he said. But he wanted nothing more than to burrow back beneath the covers all day. Now that the throbbing pain was subsiding, and the dream fragments had torn themselves apart and drifted away, a strange lethargy filled his limbs.

The air in the room grew colder and the small hairs on his arms stood up, despite being under three layers of blankets.

"Tarika?" he asked.

The bed next to him shifted and dipped, as though a person had put one knee on the mattress.

And was leaning over him.

"Oh my God," he said, willing himself to lie still. "What's happening? Who's there?"

The barest hint of heliotrope wreathed his head. And the softest whisper of lips touched his brow.

Then it was gone.

Joe found his face was wet. Tears still ran from his eyes onto the pillow beneath his head.

"I wish I knew what to do." Joe let the sadness ride his chest. Then he heard footsteps on the creaking stairs. The second one under the landing popped like a shotgun expending a shell.

Joe wiped the sheet over his face and struggled to sit up without borking his wrist again.

His brother knocked on his door. "Joe? You awake yet?"

"Come in!"

The feeling of someone else in the bed with him vanished.

Henry poked his head around the door first before stepping all the way in. He was already dressed for work in heavy tan work boots, jeans that Joe was sure had long underwear beneath them, a thermal shirt, a flannel shirt, and a red hoodie. His dark hair was pulled back into a ponytail.

"I brought you coffee, man. Figured you could use some after last night. How late were you up?"

The scent of roasted beans was a welcome distraction.

"Thanks, bro," Joe said, accepting the heavy black mug. "Too late. I had insomnia, so I'm not even sure. I couldn't stop thinking about Darius. He's kind of a mess. So I started doing some research. Trying to help him out."

"Weird. When I saw him at Constellations, he seemed okay. We talked for a few minutes. Not about anything real, you know, just chatting."

"Yeah. I think he was bluffing. He's turned into some kind of conspiracy nut or something."

Not that Joe blamed him, after some of the stuff that came up in his searches the night before. He was starting to suspect that all the fires, from all the development companies, pointed to one lawyer who worked for them all.

That was making Joe suspicious.

Henry pulled up the ladder-back chair Joe sat in when he was putting on his shoes. They sipped at their coffee for a minute. Companionable. It was the thing Joe liked most about living with his brother. The way they could just be silent together. That bugged other people.

Joe liked being quiet, though.

"What kind of conspiracy?" Henry asked finally.

"He's been tracing some connections between a bunch of major building sites all over the Pacific Northwest. Like, he thinks something shady's going on. And last night, I started looking into some of the parent companies. At least some of them are connected to that bigwig Carter."

"No shit? That guy? You remember, he outbid us for refurbishing that old Victorian apartment building about five years ago?"

"Right. I'd forgotten."

"Well, you were preoccupied with competition skate-boarding at that point. You were young, bro."

"Wasn't that young."

"Young enough to be distracted. At any rate, that guy's bad news. So, does Darius think this has to do something with Tarika?"

"Yeah."

"And you?"

"I don't know yet, man. I don't know what to think." Joe set his coffee down on his nightstand and used his right hand to adjust the pillow behind his back.

"This injury is a pain in the ass," he complained.

"Hey, could be worse. At least it's the slower season and you didn't break your neck."

"That makes me feel better."

Henry looked stared at the big casement window, covered only by a sheer white curtain. "Looks like the sun is finally coming out. Hope it stays clear today."

The two brothers drank some more coffee.

"So, besides being nice and bringing your injured brother this coffee, was there something you wanted to talk with me about?"

Henry startled from his reverie.

"Oh. Yeah. I wanted to know if the invoices on the Sullivan job were done."

"Almost. I need to track down two invoices from that one subcontractor—what was her name...Gonzales? Should have it ready by this afternoon."

"Good. I'd like to get the stuff all sent out before Christmas, if it's possible. I want all the invoices for this year to go out before year's end. And frankly, I need a break. I'm glad we don't have a lot of jobs right now."

"You ever miss Mom?"

"Every day, man. Especially right now. Think we should get a tree?"

Joe thought about it. Christmas had been his mother's favorite holiday until Dad died. That kind of ruined it for everyone.

"Yeah. Let's go pick out a tree this afternoon. You got time?"

"For you, bro? Yeah."

Henry got up to leave, then paused in the doorway.

"You think Darius is gonna be okay?"

"I have no freaking idea, bro. Dude seems seriously messed up to me. Obsessed."

Joe looked out the window at the salmon rays inching through the white sheers.

"But I can't say that I blame him."

17

CASSIEL

"Rent strike! Rent strike! Justice! Now! Justice! Now! Rent strike! Rent strike! Justice! Now! Justice! Now!"

Cassie could hear the crowd from two blocks away as she hurried, bundled up against the cold, towards city hall. She had gotten off work early and knew she needed to be out there with the crowd. The Tenants Union was calling for a rent strike, calling for justice for tenants, calling for new legislation, rent control, and tenants' rights.

She wasn't sure what good it was all going to do, or whether or not it was too late for her, which it probably was. But dammit, she decided, she was going to show up to help other people, ghosts or no ghosts, eviction or no eviction, because it was the right thing to do.

She hurried on from the bus to the curved red dome of city hall. There was a huge banner strung around the rotunda that read "Tenants Rights Now" in three-foot-tall letters. A group of about 150 to 200 people faced the rotunda under gray skies. Not a bad turnout for a weekday. They had signs, banners, placards; a small sound system was set up.

Olivia—the white woman with short, spiky black hair—was at the microphone.

"We know it's been hard on you all. We know a lot of you are tired, a lot of you are angry, and some of you may have even given up hope. Well, we want to thank you for being here, because it shows us that hope is still alive and that's what we need to be able to fight. We need everybody here and we need all your friends and families. We need renters and tenants. But you know what? We need homeowners too. Not landlords, though. We don't quite trust them."

People laughed.

"But we need regular folks. Folks who believe in community. Folks who believe that a diverse city is a good thing, not a stumbling block. And that diversity includes race, class, gender, sexuality, age, and occupation. Are you with me?"

"Yes," the crowd roared.

"Are you with me?"

"Yes," they said louder.

"All right. Well, Sharon Wilson of Justice for Portland is going to speak next, about the problems facing the black community in our city. Sharon, come up, please. Please give Sharon Wilson a hand."

Cassie had heard about Sharon Wilson; she was a firebrand and a woman who seemed tireless, at least from the outside. She was always leading something, always out on the streets or in city council meetings fighting to be heard. Cassie had to admire a person like that, although she wasn't sure how Sharon did it. Cassie couldn't quite put herself out like that.

"The African American community in Portland has been under attack for a hundred years. The whole state of Oregon used to say we couldn't live here at all, and then the white folks decided, well, maybe they needed our labor. So they let more black and brown folks move in, but we could only live in certain parts of the city, parts of the city without as many resources, without good transportation, without access. But it was a place for us to be."

Cassie looked around the crowd. Most people listened intently. There were a few people on the outer edges who seemed disgruntled, though. She wondered who they were.

Sharon was still speaking. "So we took over those neighborhoods. We bought homes, we established families, and we built businesses. We took care of each other and we took care of ourselves. We formed community. And then urban renewal happened and we all know what that's like. That means that neighborhoods that have been abandoned—all of a sudden people see they're viable and take interest and they start pouring money in. Which sounds like a good thing, until you figure out they're not giving money to the communities that have been there; they're pouring money in to attract people from outside."

"That's right, sister!" a man shouted from the front.

Sharon nodded at him, in acknowledgement, took a sip from a steel water bottle, and continued.

"We've seen it over and over again, in city after city, that this is how gentrification starts. It's taken us to where we are now—families that have been in homes for generations pushed out further and further to the edges; communities are fragmented and splintered. People move away until there's not a community anymore. There's no heartbeat. And now it's affecting even more of you. It's affecting working white folks, too, and our Asian brothers and sisters, our trans siblings, our Latinx comrades—anyone who lives on the margins is getting pushed further and further to the edge."

The scent of cigarettes floated by. That was unusual. Usually it was a tinge of marijuana that Cassie smelled around Portland artists and activists. She'd had to get used to that after moving from Tennessee. Folks didn't smoke weed in public there.

The crowd grew restless around her. She could sense it like a pressure on her temples.

"What I'm going to ask from everyone here is to stay put as much as you can. Take a stand if you can stand. Sit down if you can sit. But we need to become a force to be reckoned with. We need to become a coalition that says—enough, this stops here and this stops now!"

The crowd applauded, hooting and hollering and stamping their boots.

Olivia stepped forward again. Sharon turned and gave the slender woman a hug. Olivia took the mic.

"Thank you, Sharon." Olivia addressed the crowd again. "Some of us are calling for rent strike. I think that's a great idea. I think the more people that sign on, the more effective it's going to be. Some other comrades are also talking about squatting in some of the abandoned buildings further out, buildings they call zombie houses, that have been unloved for too long or taken over by white supremacist gangs producing meth. Some other people are calling on us to squat in some of the luxury high rises that no one can afford to move in to, take over the empty units. Why not? If they're not going to let us take care of our families, if they're not even going to raise the minimum wage to such a degree that we can afford a one-bedroom apartment, I say we take what's out there.

"If you're interested in either of these—both of which are illegal activities that I shouldn't even be talking about in public and that the Tenants Union in no way endorses—"

she grinned over the microphone "—I want you to turn to a neighbor; I want you to shake their hand; I want you to ask them if they're a cop or a federal agent."

People laughed.

"And then I want you to start planning, and know that Justice For Portland and the Tenants Union will have your backs on this, and we'll pull in the National Lawyers Guild if we need them, but I want to know who's with me. If you're with me, raise your hand."

Almost everyone there did. Cassie held back. Her heart was pounding again, but she realized that unlike last night, she didn't feel sick. She felt excited, as if maybe there was something she could do. She didn't have to be the prey of outside forces anymore.

Maybe she was in on this rent strike after all.

Slowly she raised her hand. She wondered if this was all part of what was going to make the tower fall, if it hadn't fallen already. Maybe *this* was the fire, the fire she heard in Sharon's voice, the spark she felt kindled in her own breast. She wondered, "Is this it, ghost? Is this what you want?"

"This is part of it," the voice whispered, just behind her right ear. Cassie whipped around. No one was there.

18

JOE

It was late afternoon on Wednesday and Darius had insisted on Joe meeting him at his apartment. Of course Darius lived on the third floor and there was no elevator. Joe's ankle throbbed by the time he reached apartment six and knocked on the door. Darius opened it, looking freshly washed and handsome as always. Joe could smell the man's cologne and hear the strains of Boots Riley and The Coup playing softly in the background. At least he had good taste in music.

"Come on in, man. Thanks for coming."

"Sure. Of course, Darius."

Joe limped into the room, leaning heavily on his cane. As Darius led Joe into the small living room, Joe let out a low whistle and did a slow turn, looking at all the walls.

The furniture was single-dude nice, and arranged in a typical manner: couple of black fake-leather club chairs, a nice tan, square-back sofa with red and black throw pillows. Glass-topped coffee table.

And then the incongruous walls, papered in copies of

web pages, clippings from actual newspapers. And strings and pins connecting them all.

"Darius," Joe said.

"I know, man, I know. But just look at some of it and hear me out. Okay?"

"Okay, man, but Darius, this is some crazy shit."

Every wall was covered with corkboards and white boards, covered with copies of newspaper clippings, photographs of burned-out buildings, rows of numbers, statistics. Some stuff was even drawn directly on the walls.

"Dude, what is this, like, *A Beautiful Mind*? Are you a crazy genius or something?"

"No, man, just, just wait. Just keep an open mind. You want a beer?" Darius's voice came from the small kitchen next to the living room.

"I'm gonna need a beer," Joe said. He made a note to himself that he'd pretty much had a drink every night this week and that wasn't a good road to go down. He'd start not drinking next week, he supposed. Didn't want to end up like Dad.

His eyes scanned the clippings, looked at the rows of numbers that didn't mean a thing to him. Darius walked up behind him.

"You need to get off that ankle?"

"Yeah, I do."

"Well, have a seat. We'll talk for a little bit and you can tell me what you think."

Darius seemed a little nervous, hyped up. Joe hadn't really seen him that way before. Usually Darius was Mr. Smooth. Joe felt uneasy, like, what was he even doing here, with his dead girlfriend's brother, guy who tried to beat him to a pulp and now had gone around the bend, clearly?

Joe lowered himself into the sofa and set down his cane.

He looked at the Corona Darius had handed him, then he set that down on the coffee table in front of him.

"So... Fires."

"Fires," Darius replied. "I started doing research."

"Yeah, I can see that."

"Well, I tried to put myself in Tarika's shoes, like, what would she look for, what questions would she ask."

"You have not been going around asking questions, have you?"

"No, well, maybe, not a lot."

"Oh, Darius."

"So the thing I noticed is that every couple of years there's fire like this somewhere in the Pacific Northwest—Renton, Seattle, Portland, Ashland. Anywhere there's a lot of new building going on, anywhere where there's a population explosion, either happening or about to happen. There's building and then there's fire."

"Okay," Joe said. Maybe he would need that beer. He picked it up and sipped the cool, crisp lager. Not his usual, but it was good, at least.

"Darius, you do understand that you look crazy to me?"

"Yeah, I get that. But the thing I need you to understand, man, is that my sister is dead and I've got to do something about it."

"Darius, you going crazy isn't going to bring Tarika back."

"You think I don't know that, man?" Darius got up from the chair, started pacing back and forth, running his hands across his head. "You think I don't know nothing will bring her back? You think I don't know I look crazy? But I'm telling you, man, there's something here, there's some connection, and I know she was looking into it."

"So...you definitely think someone murdered her?"

"Did suicide ever make sense to you?"

"No." Joe paused. "No, it never made sense to me. You're right. Tarika wouldn't have killed herself."

Joe felt that all the way down to his bones, and realized he *always* had felt that. It was part of what had made the grief and devastation so confusing. Her death had come completely out of nowhere.

"That's what I'm saying, man. So look, look here was this fire in Renton, here was the fire in Portland, here's one in Eugene, one up just outside of Redmond, and look, there's more."

"For how long?"

"Ten years, man. Maybe more, I'm thinking."

"Seriously?" Joe actually sat up in the couch. "Do you think there's a conspiracy about burning down building developments? And who do you think's doing it? Do you think it's anti-development people, anti-gentrification people, the developers for insurance money—you think it's arson? Have you gotten any information on that?"

Darius flopped back down on the leather chair again. "No." He leaned forward, his head in his hands, just breathing for a minute. Joe was quiet. Clearly Darius needed to think and, actually, clearly Darius just needed someone there.

"Darius, how much time have you been spending alone, man?"

Darius looked up at him. "Probably too much, but it's been hard since she passed, man. At her home-going, I could barely even look at anybody, let alone talk to anybody. Me being out in the bar this week, that was my first time out in months."

"And you had those clippings with you when you ran into me?"

"Yeah, and I don't think that was a coincidence."

"You don't?"

"I can't. I can't think anything's a coincidence right now, Joe. I have to think there's a pattern, and that pattern makes sense, and that making sense of it is going to help me figure out why my sister isn't here anymore."

Joe watched Darius pick up his own beer. He watched his throat working as he took swallow after swallow, finally setting it back down on a coaster on the coffee table.

"There's a hole in my heart, man. I don't know if you still feel it or not? But she was something good; she was better than me, better than you, smarter, stronger. I mean, don't get me wrong, she was my sister, I know she could be a bitch. There were times I wanted to whoop her ass—'course I didn't, but she and I would argue and fight. She could be selfish, you knew that."

Joe nodded. It was true she could be selfish. Although he wasn't so sure if it was selfishness so much as it was the self-centered focus of a driven person. Regardless, there were times when it felt like you might as well not even be there because Tarika was off in her own world.

"But my life isn't the same," Darius continued.

"Mine either, man. I don't know what you're doing here," Joe said. "I'm not sure that I understand, but I want you to know I'm here for you and if I can help you, I will help you, I promise."

Darius gave a short nod. Joe realized there was something else he had to come clean about.

"You know, Darius, I broke a promise to Tarika once, right before she died. I promised her six months before then that we'd talk about getting married. Three months after that, I actually proposed to her."

Darius just watched and waited.

"And I swear, man—" Joe looked down at the bottle in his hand "—two nights before she died, I called it off. Told her I wasn't ready yet. I've regretted that every day since."

"Yeah, she told me, man. She told me you broke her heart."

The words felt like a punch to Joe's chest, took all the breath out of him.

"I'm sorry she died that way," Joe said. "And I wondered if you were right, if she hadn't committed suicide because of me. If you weren't right to blame me."

"I *did* blame you, but I don't anymore. I think Tarika would have recovered. I think you both would have. I think you'd probably be getting married right now if some bastard hadn't taken her down."

"Thanks, man. If you really believe that, I think we should do our best to try and see if we can prove it."

19

CASSIEL

Cassie had stayed up late again, worrying about her housing situation, and ghosts, tarot cards, and images of fire.

Raquel had been up too, she said. Something to do with her son, Zion, having nightmares. No one was sleeping well these days, it seemed.

So here they both were, slamming through making cappuccinos and lattes, breakfast sandwiches with ham and cheese and egg on toast. People bustling in to get their go cups of coffee and scones, pastries, bananas, or yogurt and granola from the little fridge off to the side.

Cassie's bones felt as though they were moving through molasses. She kept shaking her head a little bit, breathing, trying to connect her feet to the earth below her, like a good witch. Just trying to keep up.

People seemed happy at least. That was good. It was a cheerful day, instead of a morose or cranky day. It was funny how days have personalities like that.

Cassiel, despite the disturbing visions she'd had in the night, actually felt okay. She had a lot to think about, and yeah, sure it worried her. But something else, some energy around her, was telling her things were going to be all right. It didn't quite feel like a promise, but at least it felt like a possibility.

"You almost done making that sandwich?" Raquel asked.

"Yep, coming up." Cassie slid it out of the grill, sliced it in half, two long triangles, and slipped it into a rustling white paper sleeve before handing it over to Raquel.

"Thanks." Raquel turned. "You doing okay?"

"Yeah, I'll be fine," Cassie said.

"Okay, well, we're going to have a delivery coming in soon, and I'll need you to take over the register. I'll take care of the delivery and do double duty making food. Does that sound okay?"

"Sounds good," Cassie said. That would be nice, actually. Cassie loved working the big espresso machine. She loved the hiss of the water as it steamed milk. She loved smelling the ground coffee, and seeing people's faces so grateful when she handed over their drugs.

She wondered if every drug dealer felt good about it. At least the drugs at Raquel's were benign. Although Cassie couldn't have any more espresso today or she'd shake herself to death.

"Hey, you're Cassiel, right?" It was Olivia from the Tenants Union, with her shining round face and spiky black hair.

"Yeah. And you're Olivia. Nice job at the rally in front of city hall, by the way. What can I get for you?"

"Thanks. We still have so much work to do, but that's always the way, right? Double espresso please, and the special breakfast sandwich to go."

"Coming right up." Cassie rang the woman up, took her money, put the order ticket on the rack above the counter.

Raquel started in on it; the delivery guy hadn't shown up yet.

As Cassie turned to the espresso machine, the woman looked at her phone and muttered something. Cassie usually stayed out of customers' issues, but something told her to ask.

"Pay attention to your intuition," Brenda always told her. So here it went.

She tamped the coffee grounds into the cup, slotted it in, turned the handle, and flipped the switch for the water to start moving through the grounds.

"Everything okay?" she asked.

The woman shook her head, distracted. "What? No. That bastard Carter—he's at it again."

"Carter?"

"You haven't heard? Carter's notorious. He's a big developer. Always supposed to be putting up low-income housing, and always finds some loophole, some excuse not to do it. He owns a couple of the big apartment buildings in the Northeast, a couple down by Foster. He's kicking people out again."

"Huh... I didn't think developers had anything to do with property management. I thought they all just built things."

"Well, some of them do. But some guys like Carter—they're greedy. And the greedier they are, the more pies they have fingers stuck into. So he pretty much does everything in real estate around town. He's a bigwig, has half the city council and probably Mayor Patterson in his pocket. Surprised you haven't heard of him."

"Huh... No, I haven't."

"Yeah, he's a right bastard."

Cassie handed over her sandwich and her double espresso. "Here you go."

"Thanks. Hope to see you at a Tenants Union meeting again." Olivia started to walk away and then paused. "How's your case going?"

Cassie grimaced and shook her head. "Not great. The whole building is probably going to be evicted by the end of the month unless we decide to pay the rent hike."

"Got any place to go?"

"No."

"Well, let us know if you need temporary housing. We can help."

As the woman pushed her way out the door, Cassie looked and noticed that the line had dropped down. The rush was temporarily over, at least for another half hour to an hour, which was good. She started wiping things down to get ahead on the cleaning.

Then Joe hobbled in, poor guy, and slung a heavy messenger bag into one of the empty booths along the wall. He looked haggard, with purple shadows underneath his rich brown eyes.

"Hey, Cassiel."

"You okay there, Joe?"

"Coffee please."

She smiled at his pitiful request. "Rough night?"

He looked at her. Really looked at her. It was startling to feel the gaze of his brown eyes reflecting her green. She was the one who looked away this time, picking up a rag and swiping at the clean counter.

"I did have a rough night. You look kind of tired yourself."

"Yeah. Worried about whether or not I'm going to have a place to live soon."

He took a sip of coffee, grimaced, and, leaving his cane

leaning against the counter, hobbled to the side table holding sugar and cream.

Cassie went back to work, half watching him. It seemed kind of weird that he would just walk away after she said something like that, but what did she know? She barely knew the guy.

He came back, leaning against the counter to the side of the register. A good customer, he knew not to block the place where people ordered food and drinks.

"Um…" He drank more coffee.

Cassie waited, rag in hand. Then he trained those eyes on her again. Damn it. Yeah. Weird as he was, she was definitely attracted.

"Joe, I appreciate that we're slow right now, but Raquel does still expect me to work." She smiled at him to take the sting from her words.

"So. Don't take this the wrong way. And I'm sure you have friends to stay with. People you know better…" His eyes searched her face, waiting for some sort of response.

She had no idea *what* response, though. So she shrugged, set down the rag, picked up some serving tongs and began rearranging the decimated pastry plate so it looked enticing again, rather than as if an invading horde had tramped through the bear claws and cheese danishes.

The scones were all gone, which was too bad. She'd been hoping to snag one for her break.

"So. My brother Henry and I have a big place, with an extra bedroom. And if you end up needing someplace…"

Oh. Wow. Cassie looked up again. Joe was staring into his red coffee cup, looking as if the edges of his skin were on fire, and if he could, he'd run out the door.

"That's a very nice thing to offer, Joe. Thank you so

much. I should be good for places to stay, but it's nice to know I have options if my situation drags on too long."

But I'd rather make sure you and I have a chance to wrap our arms around each other, and moving in with you and your brother might make dating a bit awkward.

"Okay. Well." He cleared his throat. "I've got some research to do, so..."

"Do you want me to carry your coffee to your table? Or your cane?"

His shoulders eased down from around his ears.

"Um. Yeah. Thank you." He handed her his cup of coffee. "I'm still not used to this. Hope I can use my wrist soon. This is a pain."

She got him settled with coffee and cane, breathing in the cool air and cypress scent of him.

"Joe?" she said.

He looked at her. Waiting. They were both waiting. She had no idea what she'd been about to say.

"Nothing. Just...thanks."

She blinked, then left him to slide a laptop from his bag and get to work.

Cassie wasn't sure exactly how she felt about a man she felt this attracted to offering her a place to stay. Not when they hadn't even been on a real date yet. It seemed like a recipe for some sort of disaster.

But maybe the universe was trying to tell her something. When one door closes and all that.

At any rate, it was nice to know that people cared.

20

JOE

Joe sighed and, swiping a hand across his face, rubbed at his eyes. They were tired and sore from looking at numbers all afternoon.

God, he didn't know how accountants did it. Just a couple of days of doing paperwork and Joe was sick and tired of it. No way. He preferred to work with his hands, his body. Sure, he needed his mind for all that: he needed to measure correctly, he needed to figure out problems, solve the mystery of what had gone wrong, put it right again. Sure he needed to be able to do some engineering. But just staring at papers...?

"How the hell do people do it?" he asked the empty room.

Henry was still out who knows where. Joe had been hoping he would come home and cook dinner. Usually that was Joe's task—he was the one who loved to cook—but with a fractured wrist, he couldn't chop a goddamn thing. He thought longingly of a vegetable curry he wanted to make. Maybe he'd order some in.

Opening his laptop back up, he searched for the food

delivery guys. Surely they had an Indian restaurant on their roster? There it was—Papadum King, just what the doctor ordered. Joe scrolled through the menu, clicked on a couple of choices, then added in some garlic naan. Jasmine rice, massaman curry with chicken, saag aloo—perfect. He called in the order and sat back in the uncomfortable office chair. That was the other problem. This chair sucked.

Well, he'd done enough for the day.

He grabbed his cane, hobbled downstairs to his favorite leather chair, and eased back down. He could sit here while he waited for the food. Unfortunately, sitting in this chair meant he started thinking of Darius.

Thinking of Darius by turns made him worried, sad, frustrated, and concerned. He still didn't know to help the guy.

"I'm sorry, Tarika, I feel like I failed you and now I feel like I'm gonna fail your brother too."

Shit. Joe couldn't figure out how he'd come to this. His life really had been simple before. Tarika was the complicated one. She used to laugh and say she loved being with him because he was so restful. He would pretend to be offended, saying she was calling him boring.

Secretly it made him feel good inside, as if he was a place for her to come to when things got to be too much.

"I wish I'd been there for you that night, baby," he said.

But he hadn't been. He couldn't have been because she wouldn't let him. That single-minded devotion to her task, that's where she was. He'd come to expect it, and gave her her space.

Except she had ended up dead from rum and pills. And no one had an inkling it was coming.

Pulling his phone out of his pocket, he thumbed

through, surfing the Internet, trying to look for some more of the connections Darius was so clear were there.

Joe began looking up some of the big developers, the big guns in Washington and Oregon, even over in Idaho. He figured they all knew each other. People at that level of business, they were always making contacts and cutting deals. Trouble was, his brain just didn't work that way—that *strings and pins on walls moving from one thing to another* way.

That was the kind of mind that Tarika had; she always saw connections.

Hmm, funny, he hadn't thought about it, but that woman, Cassiel—maybe that was what it was about her. She made connections too, but in a different way. Seemed like she made connections more with her intuition or emotions, not her mind.

"Maybe you don't know what you're talking about," Joe said out loud, "You don't even really know this woman."

His phone vibrated and pinged. A message. He looked down.

It was from Tarika's number. His breath stopped in his chest.

This time, instead of a blank message box, there was a series of numbers, which was weird.

3 4 9 6 6

Why was she sending him numbers? And how was she texting him in the first place?

Or who was texting him from her number?

And then another message box came up.

3 4 9 6 6

"What? I don't understand. Tarika..." He paused. "If this is you, and I'm not saying it is, you have to be more clear. I don't think like you and I've been staring at numbers all day now. Can you give me something else? Can you use a different keypad?"

There was a long pause. Joe started to feel kind of stupid, staring at a phone. And then there was another message box.

DIXON

Dixon? Dixon was the manager of Tarika's paper. What did Dixon have to do with anything? Then a ping, another message box.

CARTER, the message read.

Carter. "Dixon and Carter," Joe repeated.

What did Carter have to do with Dixon? And what did Carter and Dixon have to do with Tarika?

The doorbell rang; his food was here. Job hobbled to the front door without his cane, opened it onto the scent of Indian food. He tipped the delivery guy and said, "Thanks, man."

"No prob, dude." The guy ran down the front steps.

Joe hobbled back to his chair, bag of food warm in his good hand, figuring he'd just eat with the plastic fork he knew would be in the bag, even though he always asked them not to put one in. He sat down on the chair, and set the food down on the floor beside him.

"Tarika, I don't know how to do this. I'm not the person you were, but I told your brother I'd help him if I could. So if there are any clues you can give me, please let me know. Okay, babe? And Tarika, you were one of the best people I've ever known, even if you acted like an asshole when you were on a tight deadline. I hope you know that?"

He stared at the phone in his hand. It did nothing. Taking in a shuddering breath, he was about to thumb it off and put it back into his pocket when a message box popped up again.

I KNOW—it said.

Then there was another pause. His stomach growled, but he ignored it. He needed to wait and see what else the phone would say.

CASSIE KNOWS

The message box said.

"Cassie? Cassiel? Cassiel knows? Cassiel knows what? Tarika, what are you trying to say? How do you even know about her?"

Joe stared at the phone for five more minutes, listening to the refrigerator, two people talking as they hurried by outside, the sounds of a car going by, *shssssing* on the wet pavement. He didn't have that feeling of being watched, but this conversation made him want to look over his shoulder all the same.

The phone didn't reply. Maybe she was gone. Joe sighed, rubbed a hand across his face, scrubbed at his eyes again. He put the phone back in his pocket, picked up the bag of food.

"I think I need to eat something before I do something as crazy as call a chick I barely know."

His stomach cramped. No. Nervous as she made him, he needed to call Cassiel first.

He put the sack of food back down and reached for his phone.

21

CASSIEL

J oe had called her, panic in his voice, just after Cassie had pulled off her boots and started thinking about what to do for dinner.

She was exhausted, but felt compelled to slip her boots back on, order a gig car, and head out into the cold and dark. A man like Joe didn't call for help unless he really needed it.

Her ride pulled up outside a classic Craftsman. A light shone onto a stately, welcoming porch. She made her way up the walk that wound among boulders, small evergreen shrubs, and the bare branches of what looked like it might be a dogwood tree.

Cassie thanked the driver, grabbed her shoulder bag, and bundled herself up the walk.

When she found herself standing in the yellow glow of the porch light, facing the old-fashioned wooden storm door with a glass window in the top, she paused, uncertain all of a sudden. Taking a breath, she felt her intuition stir. There was something here.

She had recognized it the moment she had first seen

him, to be honest. And if they didn't have a strong connection, she wouldn't have been able to walk into what she assumed was his living room the other night.

Besides, he was Raquel's friend, and Raquel wasn't friends with untrustworthy people.

Cassiel was starting to wonder if the problem was that she didn't trust herself.

The door opened, and she saw dark eyes peering out through the glass of the storm door, and then that opened too.

"Cassiel?" he said. "Did you knock?"

"Uh, no," she replied. "I was just…"

He looked down at her boots for a moment.

"Come in." He thumped his way back, swinging the door wide as he did. Cassie couldn't believe she hadn't heard him walking across to the door with that cane.

She walked in, looking around. Sure enough, the leather recliner was there, along with a floor lamp, a few side tables, and a battered, red velvet love seat.

Just the way she'd seen them in the vision.

"Your built-ins are beautiful," she said. The tiled fireplace had a deep wooden mantle with matching glassed-in bookcases on each side.

"Yeah, isn't that sweet? You should see the built-in sideboard in the dining room. This place has the sweetest bones. We were lucky to get it."

She turned, taking in the room. The plaster was cracking in spots, needing a touchup, and one wall had a wooden baseboard stacked against it, clearly belonging to the wall opposite, where electrical work seemed to be in process.

"I like it. How long have you been working on it?"

Joe gave a short bark of a laugh. "Three years. You wouldn't know it. We fix stuff on weekends when we're not in the busy season. And, you know, other stuff takes cash, which we don't always have enough of."

Cassiel smiled at him. "Thanks again for the invitation to crash here if I need to. I can see why you love the place."

He looked startled at that. Right. He hadn't said he loved the place. But she could tell by the way he talked about it. Joe's voice had a warmth that she imagined was deadly when it was aimed at a person. A guy like him could sweep someone off her feet.

"Oh!" he said. "I'm sorry. Um, do you want to sit down? Or can I get you something to drink? I've got water, beer, or some kind of fruit juice, I think. And there's Indian food that I ordered but haven't gotten around to eating yet. We could heat it up in the microwave."

He looked at her expectantly, clearly trying to stave off talking about whatever it was that brought her there. Cassie dropped her bag on the incongruous love seat, shucked out of her coat, and said, "I'd love some food. I was just starting to think about dinner when you called."

"Okay."

"And I promise not to run out on dinner tonight."

He gave her a quick smile, and walked through the large, wood framed rectangle that divided the living room and dining room, toward a swinging door that must lead to the kitchen.

"Um, sorry it's so cold in here. We need to get the fireplace fixed. And the furnace."

"You have a lot of space, though! That's great. My place is teeny tiny. Not that I'll have it much longer, though I'm seriously thinking about joining the rent strike."

"I hate what's happening to Portland."

The kitchen wasn't in bad shape, at least. They hadn't started ripping it apart yet, not like the rest of the house.

"Me too, but since I'm part of the problem, it doesn't even feel like I get to complain. I moved here from Tennessee. Seems like everyone moves here from somewhere—except for you, I've only met a handful of other native Portlanders."

Joe started dumping the cartons into glass bowls, putting them into the microwave one at a time.

Cassie noticed he seemed relaxed for the first time around her. Which was weird, considering how freaked out his voice sounded on the phone.

"Yeah, and my family aren't natives either, that's for sure," he said. "My mother moved from Fiji when she was five, and my dad's grandparents moved here before his parents were born. I mean, everyone comes from somewhere else, right? Everyone except actual Native Americans and Native Mexicans—though I'm not sure they made it up this far."

Cassie leaned against a 1970s blue laminate counter that was clearly going to have to go when Joe and his brother got around to it.

"Well, we could talk about my housing issue and gentrification all night, Joe, but that's not why you called me."

He almost dropped the bowl he was scooping rice into. It clattered on the counter. The wary look on his face was back. Grabbing a hot pad, he dragged a bowl of what smelled like curry from the microwave and shoved the rice inside.

Then he turned, darting his glances up at Cassie's face, then back down to the floor.

It looked as if he made a decision about something, because his face changed again. He opened the old white refrigerator and pulled out two bottles of beer. Snicking off the caps, he handed her one. It was cold in her hands. Too cold. She took a quick sip and set it on the counter.

Waiting.

"Um..." Joe was back in full on nervous, shy mode. That was going to make all of this harder.

The microwave dinged. He reached in for the rice with his right hand.

"Ouch!"

Cassie gently shouldered him aside, picked up a potholder, and got the rice out on the counter as Joe ran cold water over his hand. She handed him a dishtowel as he turned, hand dripping.

"Thanks. Sorry I'm such a dork."

"No problem. Guess we'll talk about what's bugging you over food? Where are the plates?"

"Cabinet above the microwave."

She slid two blue stoneware plates out, found spoons in a drawer, and dished the food onto their plates.

"You don't have to..."

Cassie held up a hand to stop him. She was feeling impatient right about now. He'd dragged her out on a cold winter night when she hadn't had enough sleep, and was wasting her time. She didn't care how attractive he was right now.

That was weird. Cassie didn't usually feel irritated unless she was scared.

Damn it. That meant whatever it was he needed to talk to her about was no good.

It meant it was more ghost stuff.

She rattled two forks out of a drawer and sighed. She shouldn't take it out on the guy.

Her ghosts were not his fault.

22

JOE

God. He'd totally blown it. She looked pissed off and he couldn't blame her. She probably had something way better to do than babysit him tonight.

Joe followed Cassie back into the living room, ankle and wrist throbbing, singed fingers tender where they gripped the cane. As he stared at that glorious red hair, damp around the edges from the rain, his heart sank down to his toes.

Maybe it was for the best. He clearly wasn't over Tarika yet, and it seemed Tarika wasn't done with him, either, strange as that was.

Strange as everything was.

Cassie set one plate down on the side table next to his chair before setting her own plate on the long coffee table in front of the battered red velvet sofa. They really were going to have to replace that someday, or at least recover it. The thing was ridiculous. But first things first—the house needed the structural work done before anything cosmetic happened. Furniture was last on the list.

They didn't have money for it anyway. And Henry wasn't

bothered much by looks. Sure, as a builder, he loved it when things were well put together, but personally? He didn't care. He was never home to do anything but sleep these days anyway.

Whereas Joe was spending way too much time at home.

"I'll go get the beer," Cassie said, stalking back to the kitchen, boots ringing on the hardwood floors.

Joe eased himself down into the overstuffed leather chair and flipped the recliner up. He really needed to elevate his ankle. His stomach growled. He also really needed to eat.

"Here you go," Cassie said, handing him the remainder of his beer. He could smell her forest scent twining through the smells of curry and beer. He swallowed.

"Thanks."

They started eating, Joe conscious of slowing himself down so he wasn't just shoveling chicken curry into his mouth. The garlic naan was fluffy and perfect, and the saag aloo was pretty good, too.

Unlike the dinner they'd had the other night, they weren't talking. Of course, Cassie had ended up getting sick. Joe still wondered what that was about. He wouldn't think she'd freak so easily, being a witch and all.

He also wished his throat wasn't constricting with fear of talking to her about all of this stuff.

"So," she finally said, "what did you want to talk with me about?"

It really was as if she could read his mind.

He swallowed a potato. Drank some beer. Dabbed at his mouth with the paper napkin Cassie had set near his plate.

"Um," he looked down at his lap. *Get a grip, dude.* "You know how my phone freaked and I fell?"

Cassie just nodded, taking a sip from her own beer.

"Well, it's done it again. A few times. Buzzing and shaking. Not leaving a number."

He paused, took another bite of food.

"And?"

"And..." How did a person even talk about this? He looked up at Cassie, who stared at him with light gray eyes. Intent. Still a little impatience in the set of her shoulders. It also looked as if she was steeling herself for what he was going to say next. He hoped she didn't freak out again.

"Since then, they've been coming from a number. From Tarika. And she left me a message I don't understand."

The air in the room grew thick. He could hear Cassie breathing. Then he heard the pattering that signaled the rain had started up again.

"Can I show it to you?" Joe asked, fishing in his pocket for his phone.

Cassie set her plate down. Then her beer. Slowly, as if she were underwater, she rose and reached out for the phone.

"Dixon? Carter?" She looked up at him. "Who are they?"

"Dixon's her old boss. At the newspaper. Carter? Her brother found him. He's a big time builder. A real estate developer."

Cassie handed the phone back to him and sat down on the sofa, crossing her legs. They sat in silence for another moment, drinking beer.

"You think someone killed her?"

"It's starting to maybe look that way. Can you contact her or something? Or get more information?"

"You're the one with the direct line," Cassie said. Then she leaned back against the sofa and sighed, closing her eyes.

Joe just looked at her. There was tension between her

brows and a tightness around her mouth. Her fingers were tense, almost digging into the red velvet of the couch.

Finally, she sighed and opened her eyes, her face clearing slightly.

"I guess I can try doing a reading."

She dragged her black messenger bag onto the sofa and started digging through it, emerging with a purple-velvet-wrapped rectangle. She lifted her her half-empty plate off of the coffee table and set it on the floor, before her long, pale fingers drew a fat deck of cards from the purple bag.

Cassie began to shuffle. Joe caught flashes of white and bright colors. The back of the deck was a pattern of blue and green diamonds.

Cassie leaned forward and handed him the deck. "I know you can't really shuffle, with your hand and all, but just hold the cards and think of your girlfriend and what she might be trying to tell us. Cut the cards a few times, whenever it feels right. I'm going to prepare."

Slipping off her boots, Cassie tucked her feet up under her, closed her eyes, and began some deep breathing pattern.

Joe's stomach was in knots again, the naan and curry turning into a glutinous mass in his gut. He tried to match his breath with Cassiel's, but couldn't calm down enough to breathe that slowly. So he just did his best.

The cards were slick and cool under his fingers. Balancing them on his thigh, he tried to imagine Tarika, the strong planes of her face, her gorgeous curves, her laugh. The frown lines she'd get when concentrating. The cards began to tingle underneath his hand, so he cut the deck, stacking the bottom pile onto the top.

Then he cut them again, in a different place.

"*What are you trying to tell me?*" he thought. The cards hummed in answer.

He cut the deck one more time, then opened his eyes.

"I think I'm done," he said.

Cassie reached over and took the deck. She cut the deck into three piles and reconfigured them, before snapping out three cards, face down.

She turned up the first.

"The Tower," she said. "I keep getting that one, so it's not just significant to you. That represents change. Cataclysm. Rebuilding."

The hairs on the back of Joe's neck stood up. All he could think about were Darius's clippings, all the stuff tacked to the walls, the threads connecting one thing to another, like a spider's web.

"Nine of Cups reversed. Hmmm. Greed. Dissatisfaction. Materialism."

Her pale fingers turned over the final card.

"The Knight of Wands. The crusader, filled with fire." Her gray eyes stared into his own. "That sounds like your girlfriend, doesn't it?"

Joe's mouth was dry and his beer bottle was empty.

"I need another beer. You?"

Cassie sat back on the red velvet with a big exhalation, then ran a hand through her hair. "I shouldn't. Alcohol doesn't mix well with psychic work. But you know what? Screw it. Need me to get them?"

"Nah." Joe needed space. Now. Picking up his cane, he limped his way to the hulking white refrigerator, rattling in its corner. He opened the door and leaned in, letting the cool wash over his face. Sighing, he shoved a beer in his armpit under the sling and gripped the other in his cane hand.

Opener. Right. He set one of the bottles on the counter, shoved the opener in his back pocket, picked up the beer again, and headed back.

Cassie was bent over the cards again, one hand hovering just over the slick bright surfaces.

"Can you grab this?" he asked. She startled, then took the beer he gripped with his thumb, prying it slowly away from the cane.

He turned slightly. "And, sorry, but the opener is in my pocket."

She grunted and eased it out of his rear pocket. Joe just prayed his face wasn't red. *Way to think things through, man.*

"Okay," Cassie said, clearing her throat after she'd opened both their beers and Joe was settled again. "The Tower means change, but when I've gotten it recently, it was pretty clear the message was sudden change through fire. That mean anything to you?"

"Yeah. Tarika's brother...he has all these articles about fires taking out new housing developments in the Pacific Northwest. And they're all built by that dude Carter. I looked into it, and even the companies with different names trace back to him, one way or another."

"Shit," Cassie said. "Right. Carter!" She smacked a hand against her thigh. "One of my customers was just complaining about him. *He's* been setting fires?"

"It's starting to look that way; we just have to find the connections. And we're starting to wonder if Tarika wasn't onto something. And that someone killed her over it."

"Of course," Cassie murmured to herself. "Of course, it has to be ghosts again. And, oh my Goddess. How the hell did I miss that?"

Her eyes widened. "Joe, I think I've met Tarika. And I think she came to me before I even met you."

"What?" *OhmyGod, OhmyGod.* Joe's heart literally skipped a beat.

"A woman came to me on Solstice Eve. She had a pencil and a small voice recorder. A Black woman? Looked strong? And then she showed up behind me at the Tenants Union meeting. Spoke right into my ear. Said she needed my help. And to tell a man called Joe that she loved him."

Joe closed his eyes for a moment. He couldn't believe it. How was a person supposed to even process this?

When he opened his eyes again, Cassiel was holding out her hands, palms up, as if to say, *Here if you need me.* Then she raised her voice, and tilted her head up, speaking to the room. "All right, universe, I've got the message. Loud and clear. And Tarika? If you're around, I'm here to help you."

The stunned feeling in Joe's chest turned into hope. "What can you do? What can *we* do?"

Cassie took a pull from her beer. "We're going to sit here and drink beer, and you're going to tell me everything you know. Then I'm gonna have a long overdue talk with my coven, and after that? You're going to introduce me to Tarika's brother."

Joe leaned forward in his chair.

"Thank you," he said. "I can't tell you..."

Cassie nodded. "There's stuff I've been avoiding that just hit me with a clue-by-four. So it's cool. I don't have to like it, but it's cool."

Joe swallowed some more beer. Seemed like he was going to need it.

"Joe? What's Tarika's brother's name?"

"Darius."

23

CASSIEL

Cassie called Raquel and texted Selene. Those two conferred and called or texted the rest of the coven.

Everyone decided that meeting was important, and they'd change whatever plans they had to be there that night.

Walking in the fresh, cold air from Joe's to Raquel's in the light rain, Cassie shivered under the hood of her coat.

She felt almost overwhelmed with gratitude, realizing she hadn't felt safe with family in so long, not since her powers came crashing forward and changed her life. And her family had decided that the way to be supportive was to push her to help as many dead people as possible, until she broke.

Slamming herself shut had been the right answer—the only answer—but it was clear she had to deal now.

Raquel's home was in much better repair than Joe's, starting with the fresh blue paint on the porch and the brightly polished walnut of the door. Cassie raised her hand to knock, and the door swung open. It was Zion, awkwardly handsome at age almost-thirteen, wearing a Green Lantern T-shirt, jeans, and fleece-lined slippers.

"Hey Zy!" she said.

"Hey, Cassiel! Come on in. They're already in the attic. I'm just in charge of the door."

Cassie hung her coat on the row of hooks just inside the door and slipped out of her boots. Zion was already gone, heading back to who knew what computer game or book.

She exhaled, smoothing her hands over her jeans, then started up the stairs, following the rise and fall of voices. It sounded as though at least half the coven was already here. Amazing.

Cassie opened the old wood door at the top of the narrow stairs, and was greeted with a chorus and the scent of melting beeswax.

"Come in, girl. We're just waiting on Tobias. Brenda just called saying she couldn't find anyone to cover the shop, but she'd get the rundown from me or you tomorrow."

"Sounds good." Cassiel looked around slope-roofed room at the faces of her coven sitting on fat, brightly colored cushions on the white painted planks of the wood floor. Five beeswax pillars burned on a tray in the center. Most folks had mugs of tea.

"Did that son of mine offer you tea?" Raquel asked.

"That's okay. I'm full up right now. As a matter of fact, I've had two beers, which was probably not the best idea."

Raquel studied her for a moment. "As tightly wound as you've been lately? Some alcohol isn't going to hurt. We won't be working magic tonight anyway. Just talking. So, you're good."

Alejandro patted the empty green cushion between himself and Tempest. Cassie gave him a kiss on the cheek, as Tempest drew her into a sideways hug. Selene waved a beringed hand from across the room.

Cassiel burst into tears, just as another set of feet clattered up the stairs and Tobias's lanky frame burst in through the door.

"Sorry I'm late!" he said, then stopped when no one greeted him. "Oh," he said, dropping his backpack by the door and scooting onto a cushion between Raquel and Moss.

"What'd I miss?" he whispered to Moss.

"Nothing," Cassie replied. "Just me, blubbering."

Cassie pulled a handkerchief from her messenger bag and mopped her face dry.

"Thanks for coming. There's a lot going on, which I need to fill you in on, because I'm going to need your help. But first, I have a confession to make."

"May I touch your back?" Tempest asked. Always so good about checking on boundaries. Cassie nodded. The warmth of the woman's hand seeped through her sweater just between her shoulder blades, soothing her heart. Tempest was one of the coven's healers, and Cassie appreciated her skills right then.

Cassiel drew in a shuddering breath.

"I see ghosts," she said.

"You do?" Selene blurted out. Raquel shot them a look and Selene clapped a hand over their mouth.

"Let Cassie tell us what she needs to," Lucy chimed in. The house painter didn't speak often, so when she did, people listened.

"I know you all probably know about ghosts. But you don't know about *me* and ghosts, so I'm just going to start talking, okay?"

Cassie looked around the room at the candlelit faces of her friends. Her family. Tobias looked at her encouragingly.

"Sometimes there is unfinished business, and the ghost wants to make sure the living take care of things because they can't. Well, they come to me. At least they did, until I stopped them."

She leaned into Tempest's hand, feeling the soothing warmth begin to radiate outward, as the woman's gift began working its way through the layers of Cassie's aura.

"The trouble with ghosts started when I was about thirteen. Someone killed one of the teachers at my school and Mr. Ronson started appearing to me."

"Shit, that sounds intense," Moss said.

"Yeah, it was. I led the police to his killer."

"Ay diosa!" Lucy softly exclaimed.

"I know I should have told you all about this before." She looked at Selene, and then Raquel, the two people she was closer to than anyone else. She probably owed them an apology. And considering how much work Lucy did with the ancestors, she should have thought to talk with her before now, too.

"Like, I don't know why I thought a bunch of witches wouldn't understand. But it's why I left Tennessee. I couldn't stand it anymore. People found out, and everyone wanted help, and you know, I was just a kid still. Barely a teenager."

Cassie paused, taking in deep breaths. Tempest took her hand away. Cassie realized she felt a little better. As if she could do this. She could tell them what had happened.

"I kept it up all through high school. My parents insisted that I had an obligation to help all these people, and the police kept coming to me on the down low...but it got to be too much. I mean, you know what it's like to have to deal with that kind of nastiness, when all you're trying to do is figure out if you like boys or girls and if you want to go to college or not? And then the news got wind of it...."

"Damn, Cassiel," Raquel said. "I'm sorry that happened to you and you didn't have the support you needed."

"And I'm glad you found us anyway," Tobias said. "After all that? I would have told any coven to go screw themselves."

Cassie gave a little laugh. "Yeah. But I liked you guys. I guess you can see why I didn't talk about it though. At least I hope so. It took a lot to break away. And I was finally starting to feel like I was free. Like I could just study tarot cards, and work in the café...."

"And then weird shit started happening again," Selene said.

Cassiel closed her eyes for a moment, seeking out her center.

"And then I saw someone on Solstice Eve. And again at a meeting in the union hall. And then Raquel's neighbor Joe showed up at the café, needing help. Turns out the woman who's been showing up for me? It's his dead girlfriend. And we just got more information that I'm gonna need your help to take care of. If you're in."

"Just tell us what you need, mija," Alejandro said.

"Okay. So, you all know I'm getting kicked out, right? Well, turns out there's this one developer, Carter, who is doing a lot of damage right now. He's not only evicting masses of people...well, I don't have confirmation yet, but..."

Cassie gazed into the candle flames. One of the flames sputtered on the wick before flaring up, higher than the rest. The beeswax scent filled her nose.

"But the Tower is coming. And he's bringing it. On purpose."

She *knew* then. She could feel the dead woman's hand on her shoulder. She knew what Tarika wanted her to do.

"And we need to show him that he who brings the Tower, reaps the Tower."

She looked at her coven. "I need your help to take him down. With magic. Because the Tenants Union, and the newspaper, and everyone else who's been working on this? They aren't getting anywhere real. The city council doesn't seem to care. Or not enough, at least."

"These developers line government pockets. I've seen it time and again, just running my business," Raquel said. "As long as the money is flowing, it makes it hard to get anything done."

"When will you have more information?" Lucy asked, smoothing her dark hair back into a ponytail. She wound a black rubber band around the tail. Cassie swallowed a smile. Whenever Lucy was ready to work, her hair went back in that tail. It was a good sign. Meant she was on board.

"I'm meeting with Tarika's brother tomorrow, I think. Tarika's the ghost. She was a journalist and it looks like she was tracking all of this down when she died."

"How'd she die?" Selene asked, lines creasing the smooth white of her forehead.

"Pills and booze, which apparently weren't her thing. From the information she's been trying to push through from the other side, it's looking like she was murdered."

24

JOE

It was Thursday, afternoon, and gloomy outside. Everything was moving so fast, Joe felt as if he'd barely had time to sleep. Cassie had the day off and agreed to meet Tarika's brother, so here Joe was, back at Darius's apartment.

Darius's place was still kind of crazy looking. And Darius was looking ragged, as though he needed to sleep for a month. Good thing the guy worked from home, otherwise he would have been fired by now, for sure.

Darius had added more string since Joe last looked at these walls.

It was like looking at Tarika's mind in concrete form, and it made Joe wonder if their whole family thought in patterns this way.

"Wow," Cassiel said, walking from wall to wall, peering at the papers, tracing her white fingers across the connecting strands of string. "You've done a lot of work here, Darius. I'm impressed."

Joe looked at Darius, who grimaced and crossed his arms over his chest.

"Most people just think I've gone around the bend," he said.

Cassie shook her head, red hair rippling like a sun-soaked lake. "No. It doesn't look that way to me. It looks like you've been putting in a lot of research, and that you've found the easiest way to keep track of the connections your brain is making. Some people's brains like spreadsheets; other people's brains need a stronger visual. Like yours."

Darius sank onto the sofa. "Thank you. I can't tell you what a relief it is to find someone who actually understands me."

Cassie kept studying the walls. Joe paced himself just behind her, trying to see what she saw. He had a feeling she was picking up a lot more from the jumble on the walls than he was.

"Tell me what you're seeing," she said.

Darius cleared his throat. "I'm seeing...well, really, it's like an intuition I have. Tarika and I were always close, and I feel her, you know? I feel like, when I look at all this material, I see what she must have seen, and can trace her thoughts almost."

"And what's the pattern?" Cassie stopped in front of a particularly thick tangle of strings, one of the clumps Joe had seen last time that made him frankly feel worried about Darius. More strings radiated from the hub now.

That was it. It hadn't looked like a hub before, and now it was so clear, Joe wasn't sure how he had missed it.

"The pattern is fires. You see them there. Bend. Portland. Seattle. Just outside of Boise. All within the last ten years."

"The burning towers," Cassie murmured.

"What's that?" Darius asked.

"Tarot card," Joe replied. He left Cassie and sat in a chair across from Darius. "Cassiel did a reading, asking Tarika what she was trying to tell us, and a Tower struck by lightning was one of the cards."

"Huh," Darius said. "Sounds about right, though Tarika never went in for any of that shit. Excuse me, Cassiel, I don't mean any offense."

Cassie turned from the wall then, a wry grin on her face. "I'm used to it. But is tarot any stranger than you feeling your dead sister and coming up with all of this?" She gestured at the living room walls.

"No. I guess not. So what else did my sister tell you?"

Cassie finally sat down in the other chair.

"She showed us the Tower. And the Nine of Cups reversed, which is a happy merchant, with everything he needs, but reversed generally means greed and dissatisfaction. And then I pulled the image of a card I took to represent Tarika. The Knight of Wands. The fiery crusader."

Darius laughed ruefully. "That was her, all right. And I think that's what got her killed. Now I just need the proof."

He looked out the window into the nothingness of the winter dark.

"The thing I found out, following these strings? All the corporations associated with the fires had the same lawyer. So I dug some more. Turns out, they're all owned by the same man. The one you brought up the other day, Joe."

"Carter," Joe said.

"Carter," Darius confirmed.

Joe realized the apartment was pretty quiet. None of the usual neighbor noises. No television or music. You could barely even hear the cars going by outside.

It was as if a hush had stolen over the entire space. It reminded Joe of a church. Or a mausoleum.

After a moment of trying to figure out what else to say, Joe cut the silence. "Well, shit. That's what Tarika said."

Joe looked at Cassie. Her face was pale and pinched. Her grey eyes looked thoughtful.

"I think it's time you tell Darius about the ghosts, Cassie."

Cassiel stretched her arms over her head, the sleeves of her purple sweater falling down over bony wrists. She shook her hair back.

"Okay. Where to start? Ghosts... Here are the basics: if ghosts have stuck around for any length of time—and most of them don't bother, they have better things to do—sometimes our loved ones feel that we're moving on with our lives. You know, enough time has passed, we remember them, but we're just going to work every day, seeing friends, going out to the movies. All that normal life stuff. Maybe even falling in love again. Usually that makes them happy and they are able to move on too, and go where they're supposed to be next. But sometimes if something's wrong. Or if they were jealous..."

"Tarika wasn't jealous. She was never jealous," Joe said.

"Yeah. She had no need to be. You should've seen her. Tarika had it *all* going on," Darius added.

A strange look flickered across Cassiel's face. Shit. He hoped she didn't feel weird about that. Like, Cassiel was gorgeous. In a totally different way than Tarika but gorgeous all the same.

And yeah, noticing that was making Joe feel guilty as anything.

"So, when I look at these walls, and see the cards, and hear what's been happening to Joe, I think Tarika is trying to enlist our help," Cassie said. "And she's brought me to you for some reason. So after all my years of running away, it seems like I've got to start dealing with ghosts again."

Joe reached his hand across gap between the two chairs and slid his palm over her wrist, wresting on a knob of bone, fingers just touching the soft underside. He could feel her pulse, pumping blood just underneath his fingertips.

It felt right to touch her now. As if they shared a secret bond, and touching was just a physical expression of that.

"You don't have to do anything," he said. "I got this. I can help Darius. I can't do much work right now anyway. Besides, Raquel can help us. We'll figure it out."

Cassie looked at him, a light shining behind her gray eyes. She looked a little lost, but as if she was trying to be strong, too. He could see what kind of woman she must be when parts of her life weren't falling down around her head. He wondered if that was how he looked when he hadn't just fallen into a stairwell and almost broken his arm and leg.

Cassie said, "We'll figure this out. Something brought us together and I have to help you."

"I don't want you to feel like you have to do anything." Joe felt suddenly uncomfortable again. He felt Darius staring at their hands and he quickly removed his fingers from her wrist.

"I know, but that doesn't matter. I'm going to help you anyway. It's what Tarika wants." She took her eyes away from his and turned back to Darius.

"Did Joe tell you I'm getting evicted?"

Darius shook his head.

"Well, I am. And people from the Tenants Union have been complaining about this same guy. He's behind a lot of the evictions in Portland right now, and the city council doesn't seem to want to do a damn thing about it."

"So what are *we* gonna do?"

"Would you be willing to bring all your information to a Tenants Union meeting? They might be able to figure out how to take him down."

"Nah. I mean, I don't know. I don't trust groups to do it right. Too easy to infiltrate."

"So what?" Joe asked, "You going to take Carter down yourself? Challenge him to a duel? What?"

Darius shoved himself out of the chair and began to pace. "I don't know, man. I just want to blow this whole thing open, you know? I want to finish the job Tarika started."

He whirled on them both. "And I don't just want to take down Carter. I want to nail that bastard of a boss of hers, too. Dixon. She was with him the night she died and the more I research, the more I think he's in on it."

"You think he's getting paid off?" Joe asked, a chill running down his spine.

"It's starting to look that way to me. What do you think, witchy woman?"

Cassie's eyelids fluttered, as if she watched a film on the back of her eyes. Her voice changed.

"Death has come here. Seek the flame. Turn the Tower. Find the blame."

Okay. That was truly freaky. Every hair on Joe's body stood at attention. He looked at Darius, whose brown eyes were huge. The man mouthed, "What the fuck?" at him.

Joe just shrugged.

Then Cassiel shook herself. "Sorry about that. Sometimes those cantrips just come through me."

"Can-trip? What's that?" Darius asked.

"A magical poem," Cassiel replied. "It's going to help us build the spell we need to take these bastards down."

"You're in?" Joe asked, wondering what the heck Tarika had gotten him into.

"I'm in," Cassiel replied. "And so is my coven. The witches of Portland are on the job."

Huh. If a bunch of witches had his back, maybe this was going to be okay.

And all that "find the blame" business? Joe knew where to start.

25

CASSIEL

"Death has come here. Seek the flame. Turn the Tower. Find the blame," Cassie said.

"What's the rest of it?" Selene asked. They were all in black again, as usual. Today's ensemble included particularly fetching thick-soled black boots with pointed toes and silver buckles.

They were waiting for some other members of the coven in the back room of Brenda's shop on Hawthorne. The space was just big enough for the small classes Brenda, the coven, or traveling authors taught on astrology, tarot, the history of Paganism, or various magical techniques.

Mismatched wooden chairs were arranged in a rough circle. Patterned quilts hung on each wall, representing the elements. Air. Fire. Water. Earth. Bookcases crowded one corner, filled with a small lending library. A counter with tea things crouched along the opposite wall.

Cassie could hear Brenda and Tempest talking softly in the shop itself, doing all the closing-up things. Tempest would be bustling around, putting displaced items back onto their shelves, as Brenda closed out the cash register.

Tempest mostly worked as a massage therapist and healer, but she put in part-time hours at the shop for the steadiness of the few extra hours, and the employee discount on candles and herbs.

"I'm not sure yet. That was what came through. It feels like there's more, though, wanting to push its way forward."

"Well, why don't you try while we wait for the others to arrive?" Selene said. "I can scribe, if you want me to. Or make us some tea."

"You and your tea," Cassiel teased. She was filled with a sudden rush of love for her friend. What a week it had been. Meeting Joe. Solstice. The second "pay up or get out" notice. Getting contacted by ghosts again. Telling the coven. Realizing they were her new home.

And yeah, Selene. The best friend she'd wanted for a long time and never really had before because girls who talked with ghosts and helped the police track down killers were girls to be avoided.

"Thanks, Selene."

"For what? Offering to make tea?" Selene smiled, getting up and heading to the electric kettle and the mugs hanging under the wall-mounted cupboards.

"No. For being such a good friend. I never had one before."

Selene paused in the task of fishing tea bags out from the big Mason jar, but didn't turn around. "I never did, either. So we're even."

They didn't say anything for a moment, but Cassie could almost feel their breath matching across the room.

"Okay. I'm going in. If I say anything out loud, try to remember it."

"Will do."

Cassie sank her attention into her center, seeking out the

still place just beneath her solar plexus. The place her intuition lived. The place her magic rose from. Those were the first lessons she learned when she joined the coven. How to breathe properly, and how to center herself.

"Everything else flows from there," Raquel had said. Cassie hoped that was still true, even for dealing with things like ghosts and corrupt property developers, because if ever she needed to access flow, she needed it now.

Images of the tarot cards flashed through her mind. The cards from her reading with Selene, and the ones Cassie had laid out for Joe.

Then a new card insisted its way to the top of the stack. The Four of Wands. Two people celebrating in front of a castle. Structure. Home.

It would be good to have a safe space to stay, even if it was only for a while. Cassie wondered if she would still need to fight for her apartment if they figured out how to take Carter down. Who knew what cascade of dominoes might happen in Portland after that?

She swept the thought aside and deepened her breath again.

"Show me," she whispered. "Tell me."

"Death has come here. Seek the flame. Turn the Tower. Find the blame."

Turn the Tower. What did that mean? Was it like turning the tables, or like, look in a different place?

"Take up the task. Unveil the mask..." she said out loud, as the new words tumbled into her heart and mind. "Seek out the one who hides the text. He points the finger, knows what's next."

Cassiel waited. Listening for more. The energy around her settled, signaling that the transmission was done, and she came back into the room, to the warm scent of turmeric tea with honey, and the sound of Selene scratching words into a notebook with their favorite fountain pen.

She knew her words would be set down in lavender ink on unlined pages. That was just how Selene rolled.

The room felt full. Sure enough, as she looked around, she saw Brenda and Tempest, Moss, Alejandro, Raquel, Lucy, and Tobias.

Tears pricked at the back of her eyes. They had all showed up. For her. Again.

What did she do to deserve this?

"Got it," Selene said, setting down the pen. "Any clue what it means?"

Cassie rubbed her eyes and took a sip of tea. It was good. Smooth. Slightly nutty and a little sweet.

"As a matter of fact, yes. I think it means Tarika's boss was covering a lot of shit up. 'Hide the text.' That would be Dixon, and I swear to all the Gods that his finger points directly to Carter. Tarika was pretty clear about that, and all the evidence her brother gathered points that way."

"So what are we going to do?" Moss asked, his serious face a stark contrast with the bright yellow "I'm not your Asian sidekick" T-shirt he wore under an unbuttoned black sweater.

"I'm hoping you all can help me craft some magic to take these people down. Or at least..." Cassie thought for a moment. "When I was inside just now, those words about 'unveil the mask' really stood out, almost like they were limned with light. So maybe that's what we focus on."

"Anyone have a clue what that means? Any hits?" Brenda looked around the room. Cassie did, too. Everyone was silent, sipping tea, or eyes closed, clearly listening for information from the other planes. Lucy paced near the door to the shop, clearly too restless to sit. Tobias leaned against the wall opposite Cassie.

The scratch of Selene's fountain pen was joined by the sudden tap tapping of rain. Selene looked as though they were sketching something.

Tempest cleared her throat. "The only hit I'm getting so far is a desperate sense from...the city itself. Like it needs healing. But that doesn't seem like it helps us much."

Lucy stopped pacing and spoke. "I don't think that's true. It feels to me like that sense is at the heart of what we're dealing with. It's always good to name the underlying condition, right?" She held out her hands, as if she could feel the air in the room. "If the dead want something from us, and the city wants something from us, those are two different directions to look from. It feels as if there's a third. Anyone getting it?"

Tobias pushed off from the wall and stood up straight. "The thing I'm getting is a sense of rage about all of it, and I don't know if that's just from me, or from something or someone else."

"Let's all see if we can tune into that," Raquel instructed, adjusting her posture on the folding chair. Cassie noticed that she made sure her feet were flat on the floor. Cassie unfolded her own legs. Sure enough, the energy shifted. It felt as though things flowed more smoothly. Clearly.

A question emerged in her mind.

"You know, I think there are a lot of scared and angry people in this city right now. I know there are. And Tarika, the ghost, is angry. But..." Cassie closed her eyes and slowed her breathing down. Reached for the threads that were floating just beyond her awareness. Grabbed ahold. Her eyes snapped back open.

"I think the developers are angry, too. Especially Carter.

And if that's the case, the empaths in the room should be able to tap into that, and trace the emotions back to the source."

"And that will give us the in for whatever magic we decide to do," Brenda said.

Raquel nodded. "Good work, people. We're one step closer. But we still need to figure out exactly *what* to do, and we haven't done magic this big in a long while. Since before you joined us, Cassiel."

"Well, it's clearly time," Moss said. "There are a lot of things that need fixing, and if we're not going to try, who is?"

Cassiel found herself agreeing, for the first time since she'd fled Tennessee and all of those murdered people. If not her, who?

She just hoped that helping ghosts wasn't going to turn into a full time job.

Joe didn't feel ready for this, but he figured he never would.

He didn't want anyone to talk him out of it, talk him into waiting, talk him into getting back up.

So he was hobbling down the damp sidewalk in the early winter dark, passing two houseless people huddling under a building overhang, trying to stay out of the rain. Passing the coffee shop with steamed-up windows and warm lights. A place he would rather step into, rest his aching ankle and wrists. Sip some coffee. Read a book.

Instead, he was headed toward the two-story brick building just up ahead with an incongruous red Triumph Spitfire parked out front.

The *Mount Tabor Monthly*. He wasn't even sure they'd still be open, but knowing it was the end of the month, and there was a holiday coming up, he was banking on them working overtime, trying to get next month's issue ready for press.

After meeting with Darius and Cassiel, he felt sufficiently angry to do something stupid, and the pain in his body only ratcheted up his sense of irritation and injustice.

"We're gonna get him, Tarika."

And then he was at the wooden door. Slipping his cane over his right forearm, Joe opened the door. He was assaulted with the scent of fresh ink from the pile of papers near the door.

The sound of clattering computer keys and several telephone conversations at once filled the air.

A skinny white dude with a dark beard and an orange plaid flannel shirt sat at the wooden counter that separated a small waiting area with battered gray chairs from the rest of the open office space. He was reading the paper and eating what smelled like a roast beef sandwich. Joe's stomach growled.

The man set his sandwich down and wiped his face and hands on a paper napkin.

"Sorry. No one's available to spell me for a dinner break. May I help you?"

"I'm here to see Dixon," Joe replied.

"Do you have an appointment?" The man turned to the computer next to him and clicked, looking at the screen.

"Not really."

A frown appeared between the mustache and beard. "Well...I can see if he has time, but we're in a production crunch right now."

"That's okay, I'll just head on back."

Joe moved forward, pushing open the half-height swinging door with his cane. He hobbled as quickly as he could down the center aisle between the rows of desks. His sights were set on the wooden door at the end, set with opaque glass at the top. Peeling gold leaf read "Editor" on the glass.

"You can't…"

Joe heard the man sigh.

"Okay. I'm calling him," the man said.

The aisle seemed as if it went on forever, even though the room wasn't that long. Funny what happened to space and time when your body was injured. Distances seemed longer and things took twice as long as you wanted them to.

Joe heard a muffled voice behind the door, slung his cane under his arm, and turned the old brass knob.

Dixon sat behind an ancient, heavy wooden desk piled with paper, a computer monitor hulking in one corner.

"Thank you," he said into his phone, then clicked it off and stared at Joe from behind a pair of retro tortoiseshell-framed glasses that he'd likely had since they were hip the first time around. He wore a white button-down shirt rolled up to the elbows. The office was pleasantly warm.

"Who the hell are you?" Dixon asked.

Joe levered himself down into the green padded chair facing Dixon's desk. Just looking at the man filled him with the prickling of rage.

"My name is Joe. And I'm your conscience."

Dixon pursed his lips.

Joe waited.

"What the hell is that supposed to mean?"

"It means I think you've been up to some pretty shady dealings, Mr. Dixon. And the piper is wanting to be paid."

Dixon's fingers tapped on the desk top as if he were jonesing for a cigarette but had quit too long ago to have a spare pack hidden in his desk drawers. He stared at Joe, expressions flicking across his face. Joe could tell he was trying to figure him out. And that he was annoyed.

Well, that was just fine. Joe was more than annoyed, and anger trumped annoyance every time. Joe looked around the room at framed photographs of Dixon with local politicians, Dixon in a sculpture garden, a photo of the city skyline, shot across the Willamette.

And a photo of Dixon and Carter, golfing with Mayor Patterson. Bingo.

"I still don't know what you're talking about, but I have a newspaper to get out, so I'd appreciate you leaving my office."

"I'm sure you would. And I would appreciate my girlfriend still being alive."

For one moment, Dixon looked as though he'd been slapped, before he schooled his face back into more even planes.

Joe practically tasted blood in his mouth, as though he'd bitten the man. He wanted to bite the man, that was for sure. Bastard.

He leaned back in his chair, glancing at the photo of the developer and the newspaper editor, then back to the editor himself.

"Why is it that your paper has never published anything other than puff pieces on Carter?"

"Carter? What does Carter have to do with anything? And who the hell is your girlfriend?"

Dixon swiped a finger across his upper lip. Good. He was sweating.

Joe leaned forward, blocking out the sounds of the office outside the door, focusing on the breath wheezing out of Dixon's lungs. He wished for a moment that he had some sort of magic powers. He didn't. But he knew things that could ruin this man, and he wanted Dixon to know it.

"I think you're in Carter's pocket. He either has something on you, or he paid for that sweet old Triumph Spitfire I saw parked outside. You don't look like you can work on it yourself, and I know the editor of the *Mount Tabor Monthly* can't afford the upkeep on a classic car like that."

"You're full of shit," Dixon said. He shoved his chair back and stood, leaning over the desk. "I don't know why you're hurling these accusations, but I need you to leave now."

Dixon practically flung himself around the desk, en route to the door.

"Tarika Henderson," Joe said, watching the man's face carefully.

His face spasmed and Dixon stopped, breath coming more quickly. He licked his lips.

"Tragic death," Dixon said. "We never suspected she had such...issues."

Joe slammed his cane on the floor. "You *know* she didn't have 'such issues.' You *did* something to her. Did you hire someone to drug her rum? Did Carter? She had a whole raft of information on the two of you. Enough to take you down."

Dixon's face hardened. He was silent. Joe smelled the stink of fear on the man and stifled a smile. He waited.

"I have no idea what you're talking about," Dixon finally said. "And I need you to leave. Right now."

He opened the door.

Joe sat for another moment, just looking at the man. He didn't look well at all. Sweaty. Slightly gray.

Despite the posture of challenge, Dixon's eyes looked wary. A little scared.

Gripping his cane, and forcing himself to not wince, Joe levered himself back up from the chair.

"Happy to leave. I delivered the message I was entrusted with."

He paused when he reached the door, so close to Dixon

he could kiss him. Or punch him. But that would ruin his one good hand.

And Joe's job today wasn't to deliver justice, it was to move a few more chess pieces into place on the board.

"Who is this message from?" Dixon couldn't help himself. He had to ask. Just as Joe had planned.

"A group of very powerful people that you really shouldn't have messed with. Oh, by the way, Tarika says hello."

Joe limped out through the door. He could feel Dixon standing behind him still. Watching him walk away.

27

CASSIEL

Cassie lay on the floor of the shop. It had grown late. She was tired from the meeting, tired from thinking, exhausted from the emotional output. She so wasn't used to this anymore. She'd grown used to feeling almost normal.

But they weren't done yet. Cassie tried to force herself to relax. She did that old trick of tensing up every muscle and then letting go. She tried to drop her attention into her solar plexus.

Tried to slow her breathing down.

"Stop fighting it, Cassiel." Brenda's voice penetrated her struggle. She felt a light touch on her forehead and her belly. "Go deeper."

Cassie took in a halting breath and spoke. "The ghosts..."

"The ghosts are fine." That was Raquel's voice. "*You're* fine. You've got this, and *we've* got *you*."

Cassie felt the coven around her, felt the caring and solidity of her coven mates, smelled the comforting scents of beeswax and frankincense. It reminded her that, even though her housing was in danger, there was still a place where she could feel a sense of home.

She listened to Brenda's voice starting over, guiding her into deeper states of relaxation.

"Slow your breathing down," her mentor said. Finally, Cassie could feel her body respond to the words; she could feel her diaphragm and her belly expanding, then her lungs. She could feel as every member of the coven around her also deepened their inhalation. It was as though the whole room inhaled, paused, exhaled and sank a level deeper.

Cassie let her attention drop deep into her belly, with a flicker of awareness that it felt easy this time.

"Take another breath," Brenda said. Cassie felt the rough nap of the rug underneath her fingertips. She settled more deeply onto the rug.

"Imagine you're floating," Brenda continued. "Imagine you're floating on a red cloud."

Cassie let her mind follow the voice and let the familiar imagery of the different colored clouds wash through her from red to orange to yellow to green to blue to indigo, and on to a deep, rich violet.

"And step out of your body," Brenda's voice continued, "and look around. What do you see?"

Cassie saw her place of power, the place that felt like her safest center, the place where she was most herself. But she knew that this outcrop of rocks in the north and the sun setting over the ocean in the west—they were not where she was supposed to remain. This was really the starting point, the place to begin.

She turned, looking in each direction, and then she saw it—her guide, a small hummingbird, tracing a pattern in the air, and yes, there it was, just beyond the hummingbird—a shimmering doorway. As she walked towards it, the doorway solidified into a slab of blond wood inset with a window. She heard the clattering of computer keys. She smelled ink and paper and a hint of old cigars.

Cassie walked towards the door, put her hand on the brass knob, and opened the door. This must be Dixon, Tarika's old boss. She looked at him. There wasn't the energy around him that said he was the one she was seeking. She shut the door and backed away.

"Show me someplace else," she murmured. She turned, and the hummingbird was right in front of her, startling her. She took a step back, hand flying to her chest.

"Can you tell me where to go? I think I'm looking for this man named Carter," she said, "or some of his associates. We need more information please. Show me."

And all of a sudden, Cassie dropped through several layers, worlds upon worlds whirling around her. She was spinning. She felt like she wanted to throw up. She tried to gasp a breath, and finally—*bam!*—she slammed down onto a piece of tarmac, the feel of gravel digging into her palms and her cheek.

"Okay, that was not what I expected," she said. Struggling to sit up, she looked around. She was just outside a building site construction area. There were large metal scaffolds, metal beams, poured concrete with rebar sticking up, and wooden walls rising all around her.

Sure enough, there was a big blue sign with yellow letters. "Carter," the big yellow letters read. Next to the name was a large, spoked wagon wheel. A play on the company name. Carter. Maker of carts. Transporter of goods.

And then the smell hit her. Not only the construction smells, concrete and wood, machinery, oil, but the acrid scent of spilled gasoline. The fumes grew more pungent. She fought to not gag, put a hand to her face and breathed deep, reminding herself she wasn't really here; this wasn't going to affect her body.

"Calm down," she said. "Your body can take a breath. You're just seeing what was."

That was clear. Cassiel knew, somehow, that this was the past, not the present.

Where was the smell coming from? She let herself float up, trying to get a better vantage point, quicker than walking. She slid over the building, over the construction site and looked down.

There they were—two figures in hooded sweatshirts. Looked like men. They were dumping...a different scent, maybe kerosene? She wasn't sure. They'd opened up one of the machines and were letting the gas just pour out of it. It ran, a dark and spreading river, across the site.

"Let's go," she heard one of them say, and the two men ran. As they ran, boots crunching gravel, one of them threw a match over his shoulder and the place burst into flames.

Cassie slammed back into her body, gasping. Heaving breath into her lungs, she felt a cool hand on her forehead.

"Slow your breathing down, Cassie. Cassiel, slow your breath." Brenda's voice again. And then two warm hands around her ankles. She couldn't tell who it was, but it was clearly one of the healers.

She fought the wish to exit her body again. She fought the panic. She fought to get her mouth and lungs and nose working again.

And there, finally, her breath caught. She relaxed her spasming diaphragm, and took in air again.

"That's good," Brenda's voice said. She felt the healer down at her feet, drawing her spirit back, all the way to her toes. That helped too.

Cassie felt the crick in her neck. She felt the carpet

under her fingers again. But she also still felt the vestiges of the pain from her hands smacking tarmac and pebbles, and she tasted blood where she must have bit the inside of her cheek from the fall. Her nostrils felt singed from the fumes, though her mind tried to tell her that wasn't possible.

The spiritual impacts the physical. That was one of the first lessons the coven had taught her. She guessed it was true.

"Can you sit up? Drink some water?" Selene's voice came from above. Cassie could smell the water in their hands.

"Yes," she croaked out. Arms, hands, helped her sit up. She opened her eyes finally, and looked at Selene's beautiful eyes. She reached out, took the cup of water from her friend's hands, and drank. Nothing had ever tasted so delicious.

"Okay, do you want to stay on the floor, or do you want a chair?"

"Chair, I think," Cassie said, handing the cup of water back to Selene. Brenda and Tobias helped her up, got her to a chair.

Raquel sat down next to her and put a hand at the back of her neck, keeping her grounded. "Take another few deep breaths, girl," Raquel said, "and then tell us what you saw."

28

JOE

"How's it going with your woman, bro? You can't hold out on me forever."

Joe was back home, specifically not talking with his brother about confronting Dixon. He wasn't ready to. Not yet.

He and Henry were decorating the little fir tree Henry had brought home after he cut out on his last job for the day. Joe loved the balsam scent.

It filled the aching he'd carried for the past year. Soothed it.

Joe worked at untangling the hooks in a box of bright glass Christmas balls as Henry untangled the cords of lights.

"Why don't we put this shit away better?" Joe asked.

"Because we're lazy about everything except our tools," Henry replied. "And don't weasel out of answering my question. You've had a lot on your mind lately, and not just the weird stuff with Tarika and Darius."

"Speak for yourself, man. My room is always clean, and I'm forever cleaning the kitchen after you, too. Slob."

"And...?" Henry had gotten the small colored lights

straightened out and began winding them around the branches.

"And...Cassiel isn't my woman, and we've barely had a date."

"You had a date? I *knew* it! I knew she wasn't just 'helping you and Darius out'. What happened? Any other dates in the future?"

Joe stood up, carefully balancing a box of half a dozen ornaments in his good arm, and hobbled, caneless, to the tree. Then realized he couldn't hold the ornament box and hang the ornaments at the same time.

"Get me a folding table?"

Henry looked at him and gave a short laugh. "Sure."

All set up, Joe brought a couple more boxes over and started hanging the gold, red, and blue glass balls on the upper branches as Henry plugged in the lights.

The colored lights reflected off the bulbs and refracted from the white walls, warming up the stark room. Joe couldn't wait until they could actually decorate, but with all the remodeling they still had to do, it was useless to even try.

Henry cleared his throat. Waiting.

"Well, we sort of had a date...we went out to dinner, but she got sick and had to leave."

"You're kidding me? That must be the worst first date you've ever had."

"No kidding. Not that I'm even sure that was a real date. I mean, I wanted to discuss Tarika with her...."

"Smooth, man. Inviting the hot new woman to dinner to discuss your dead ex."

Joe winced and dropped a bulb. The delicate glass shattered on the floor, breaking into four big golden pieces.

Henry looked up from unpacking another box of ornaments, this one a mix of small wooden toys and woven grasses tied with ribbons. Childhood stuff.

"Sorry, man. I didn't mean it. Shouldn't have said that." He hurried over to pick the pieces up and threw them in a waiting trash can.

Joe shrugged and blinked back the tears that had shocked his eyes. He picked up a red ornament and hooked it onto a branch.

"At any rate, we haven't had time to have another date since. Just ate dinner here one night, and then I've taken her over to meet Darius."

Henry paused. Then sniffed the air.

"What's up?" Joe asked.

Henry held up a hand, then moved away from the tree, still sniffing.

"You smell gasoline?" he asked.

Then it hit Joe's nostrils, the acrid, searing scent of it.

"Shit! Yes!"

Henry ran to the front door. Joe heard it wrench open. A rush of icy air whipped into the room, bringing the scent of gasoline with it.

"Get the fuck out of here!" he heard Henry yelling, followed by a flash of light and the sound of boots striking the sidewalk.

Joe grabbed his cane and moved as quickly as he could to the porch. Two hooded figures ran from their yard, followed by Henry. The scent of gas was strong.

"What the hell?" Joe asked.

The porch light on the Craftsman next door click on and their neighbor, Jack, came out onto his porch, dragging a jacket on.

"What's going on?" Jack called.

"I think two assholes just tried to torch our house!" Joe said.

Ice climbed up Joe's spine as soon as the words left his mouth. He started shaking so hard it practically knocked the cane from his hand. It had nothing to do with the wind.

Then a flash of heat moved through, taking over his whole body in a rush.

Joe was angry. So angry. He wanted to take his cane and smash whoever this was. Whoever had dared to come threaten their home.

Jack loped across the dried-out lawn, past the big, bare maple tree.

"You gonna call the cops?"

"What?" Joe looked at his neighbor, face half in shadow, half lit by the light streaming from the open door. "I...I don't know. I guess so."

"You do that, and I'll get a flashlight and start checking around the house."

Joe slipped his phone from his pants pocket and paused. "If I'm calling the cops, won't you walking around mess up, I don't know, footprints or something?"

Jack stopped. "You're probably right. Can we at least turn on your outside lights?"

Joe told him where the switch was and had just dialed the local station when Henry came huffing back up the sidewalk.

"Lost them," he said, as he walked, breath heaving, up to Joe. Joe held up a hand. Someone had answered.

He called in the attempted arson as Henry went to talk to Jack.

Lights flooded the yard. Henry had turned on the porch light and the side security lights that had come with the house and they never turned on because they shone into the neighbors on either side and they wanted to keep Jack and Raquel around.

"What'd the cops say?" Jack asked.

"They said we need to call the fire department, and to not touch anything. To take pictures of anything obvious, though. They'll make sure a patrol car makes regular passes tonight."

Henry nodded and waggled the phone in his right hand. "I got a picture of the two guys, too. Probably not faces, but one of them did turn to look at me when I ran out." He thumbed through the photos. "Gotcha, asshole."

"Really?" Jack asked.

Henry turned the phone toward them. Joe could see one of the guy's faces. White guy, mid-thirties, maybe. Strong face. Dark eyes. Looked like a broken nose.

"Why the hell would anyone want to set your house on fire?" Jack asked Henry as they walked off around the side of the house, where the gas smell was strongest. Joe eased himself down onto the porch steps to call the fire station.

Joe saw more flashes. That's what he had seen before. Henry taking a photograph.

As Joe looked up the number for the closest station, he felt the embers of his anger resurge.

He knew exactly who would want to set his home on fire.

He wondered if there was any way to prove it.

Instead of the fire station, he looked up the *Mount Tabor Monthly* and began to punch the number in.

Right before he pressed the dial button, he stopped himself. "Don't be an idiot, Joe. The less Dixon knows you know, the better."

He called the fire station instead. They said that yes, the police were right, and they should take photos. Since nothing had been lit on fire, an investigator would be over in the morning.

But Dixon had something coming to him, that was for sure. As soon as Joe figured out how to pin it on him.

Dixon and that bastard, Carter.

29

CASSIEL

The coven adjourned to Sub Rosa for margaritas and nachos, deciding they all needed a break.

Sub Rosa was a funky neighborhood place owned by one actual Mexican dude and a couple of his white, hipster friends. The walls were painted chili pepper red, and the seating was a mix of old 1950s kitchen chairs and padded pews reclaimed from a Baptist church in Lincoln City.

As with so many neighborhood places, the art rotated. This month's display was a collection of cool papier-mâché masks.

Cassie was still a little bewildered, a little out there. Both Brenda and Raquel insisted that tonight, alcohol would bring her all the way back most quickly. Tempest and Tobias, the two healers of the group, concurred.

It wasn't the best or safest way to come back, but sometimes under stress, it didn't hurt.

Some old Arcade Fire pumped through the speakers above their table, adding to the noise of the late-night crowd.

Cassie scooped up some black beans and cheese on a

crisp tortilla chip and shoved half of it in her mouth, crunching down, trying to catch the beans that fell before they hit her lap. Selene handed her a napkin. Cassie nodded thanks as she chewed. Oh yeah, protein was the best, even better than the alcohol.

A body needed protein to come all the way back from the other realms—beans and cheese, a little bit of grease, that would do just fine. She grabbed another chip and dipped it in some guacamole, letting the avocado and salsa taste chase the black beans and cheese down.

"Keep eating," Raquel said.

Cassie chewed and nodded, giving her friend and boss a small smile. Then she picked up her margarita, finally, put her lips around the salty rim, and took a drink. She winced a little at the tart lime, but then the sweetness hit her and the taste of tequila ran warm down her throat.

Margaritas were usually a summer beverage, but she figured if a place *made* them in late December, she could *drink* them in late December. She was uncertain about the avocados, though. Avocados and tomatoes were way out of season.

"So, what kind of magic is going to take this dude out?" Moss asked.

Cassie shook her head, hoping someone else had an answer, because she surely didn't—not yet, at least.

"Well, think about Cassiel's cantrip," Lucy said. "She talked about a mask, right? Unmasking?"

"Yes."

Selene looked at her notes, and began to recite the spell.

"Death has come here. Seek the flame. Turn the Tower. Find the blame. Take up the task. Unveil the mask..."

Cassie looked around, making sure that no one at any of the other tables could hear. Sub Rosa wasn't too crowded; it was just crowded enough that there was enough noise to mask any of their conversation if they kept it low, and the two tables nearest them were empty, thank the Gods.

"It's okay, we checked," Brenda said, laying a hand on her wrist. "Just keep eating."

"I will," Cassie said, drinking more margarita, "I will."

Selene continued. "Seek out the one who hides the text. He points the finger, knows what's next."

Cassie tried to ignore the aching at the base of her skull that just hearing those words brought on. She scooped up more food and looked around at the Coven of the Arrow and Crescent, filled with a sudden surge of love. They all had their own lives, their own troubles, she knew it, but they also were all committed to helping whoever needed it.

It was part of why she had joined. They weren't just about spiritual work; this coven was about service. Cassie realized all of a sudden that was important to her. But she was still thinking too much and not eating or drinking enough.

She took another sip of her margarita on the rocks and then shoveled more nachos into her mouth. "So, it seems like we need to do some magic to unmask him?"

"Yeah, but what's that gonna look like?" Tobias asked, running a hand through his dark sweep of hair.

"I'm not sure how we're going to get that done," Brenda replied, bracelets clattering as she picked up her glass of pinot noir. "Anyone have ideas?"

The whole coven sat for a moment. The only sounds were conversations from the other tables, the old Iggy Pop that had replaced the Arcade Fire, the crunching of chips, and the sipping of drinks.

That was fine with Cassiel; she still needed some space.

She was still reorienting herself. Just over a year into coven work, she was still new to all this astral travel and trance work. She'd been told she'd get better at it and it would get easier over time, but this was still the longest, most intense trip she'd taken, and she'd frankly never tried to go any place real before, at least not ordinary world real. She had really only traveled to her place of power and, a couple times, and taken a trip to a few of the astral realms, always led by one of the coven members.

This had been her first time flying solo, so to speak, with no one coming with her into the other realms. She took another sip of margarita, rolling an ice chip around in her mouth and then swallowing. Her hands smelled of black beans and tequila.

"I think I know," she said. Somewhere between sipping and swallowing, an idea had formed in her head. "I think it's a two-pronged attack. I think we cook up some way to do the unmasking, right? Some magical thing, and I don't know how that works; I'm hoping some of you do. But, simultaneously we find a big event Carter's going to be at—and they're always happening; the man loves to style himself a philanthropist."

"That's the truth," Moss said. "That dude is always getting his face in the paper, he's always out there gladhanding, shaking hands and messing over the poor."

"That's the MO of so many people," Lucy said. "I'm sick of it."

"Okay everybody, give Cassie a chance here," said Raquel, always the voice of reason.

"So, we find a way to work some magical unmasking, do some energetic work around the guy. I don't know, maybe around his name, his symbol, right? His corporate brand. We can do that kind of work, right?"

"Hell, yes," Alejandro said. "Sigil magic is my main jam. I can do anything with that."

"Good. Next is to pick a time and a place, and send in Joe and Darius."

"Send in Joe and Darius with what?" a man's voice said.

Cassie's head whipped around, and there was Joe, looking gorgeous and concerned, with two other men behind him.

"Joe!" she said. "What are you doing here?"

"Henry and Jack!" Raquel said.

Joe caned his way forward. "Sounds like we need to be part of whatever conversation you're having.

Cassie caught Raquel cheating Joe a look.

"It's okay, Raquel, we filled Jack in on some of it earlier. We had to explain it after two guys tried to torch our house tonight."

"What?"

Some of Cassie's coven mates were already shoving chairs around and pulling another table over. It was clear the meeting they needed to have was going to happen now.

"While everyone get's themselves settled, you need to eat more nachos," Raquel said to Cassie before turning back to Joe. "What's this about your house?"

Cassiel shoved another loaded chip into her face just as Joe pulled up a chair next to her.

She tried not to blush, and failed. Damn pale skin.

"It's part of the larger conversation we all clearly need to have here," Joe said. "I can't imagine that researching arson and having two dudes pouring gasoline around our home are unrelated. At any rate, we'll know more tomorrow, after the fire marshal comes. They said they couldn't investigate properly tonight anyway."

The waitress came back then, and asked Jack and Henry what they wanted.

Cassiel was staring at Joe. Stunned that he was in danger. She didn't want him to be in danger. He caught her staring and smiled.

"Hey there," he said. "How are you?"

Cassie coughed, took another sip of tequila and lime, and looked into his brown eyes.

"I think I'm going to be okay. But I should really ask, how are *you*? That's so scary!"

"Pissed off. But better now. I called Darius about it. He's on his way here now."

He held her gaze for a moment. Cassiel could practically feel the heat crawling up his skin, but his eyes didn't look away.

"Cassiel?" he asked.

"Yes?"

"When all of this weirdness is over, would you go on an actual date with me?"

A short, surprised laugh almost made her spill what was left of her margarita.

"Yes. Yes I would. That sounds great, Joe."

He snaked his uninjured hand over, and Cassie took her own hand from around her glass to met his. Cool met warm. It felt good. Right. Like a mug of hot chocolate on a cold day.

And it made her want more.

Joe flashed her a slight smile, and gave Cassie's fingers a squeeze before turning his attention to the waitress hovering over his shoulder.

Yeah. It actually did sound great. Both the weirdness being over, and a date with Joe.

30

JOE

Darius, Joe, Henry, and Jack had all agreed to do this crazy thing. To work with a coven of witches to blow apart a possible corruption scandal holding the city of Portland hostage.

Why the hell not? Right? Keep Portland Weird was an empty slogan if people weren't willing to *actually* do weird shit.

The brick façade of the museum was all lit up. Lights shone on the roof to sidewalk banners of the latest exhibition of Native American textiles and fashion. The glittering crowd of Multnomah County's wealthy patrons hadn't begun to arrive, but the staff were already inside, setting up.

The streets were fairly deserted. Not too many people were in downtown Portland on Christmas Eve. Only those who couldn't afford to take the night off, or those who were so wealthy, they didn't need to worry about what night it was, or those who didn't have a warm place to go home to.

Joe had wanted to be in position, to scope the museum corner out. He needed to figure out where the best place was to stand until it was time to take advantage of the photographers and society reporters who would be covering the event.

The coven had been pretty clear about one thing. They couldn't let Carter get inside the building before confronting him. As soon as he was behind the big glass doors, they would lose him for hours, by which time the outside news crews would have long gone.

An invitation-only event starting at two grand a ticket was as good as a crenellated fortress with a reinforced drawbridge and a moat.

And last Joe had checked, he was a twenty-five-year-old Melanesian geek with a busted ankle, not Spiderman.

Besides, to do the unmasking, Cassiel insisted that they needed the bright lights and flash of the news. Joe knew that from experience, and from his little encounter with Dixon. To take down men like this? If you didn't have pockets and connections that went much deeper than theirs, you needed the power of the press, dubious as it might be.

If the story was big enough, it would spread from the society pages to the front page, above the fold. All it needed was a reporter interested enough—and with enough footwork already done—to get it into their teeth.

"Tarika, if you've got any help to give me, now's the time. I know you worked hard on this story. Let's break it wide open? Whisper into one of your colleague's ears, okay?"

The snowflake touch of her hand replied. God, he still missed her. Tarika had really been something special.

He was thinking Cassiel might be that special as well. She had told him to think of her and to imagine that they could connect "by the power of thought." He wasn't sure about that, but figured it was worth the try.

She certainly seemed worth the try.

It was colder than it had been, just the day before. For

sure another round of snow was on the way. He tugged at his watch cap with his good hand. Henry was a few feet away, talking quietly into his phone. Jack was parking the car.

If it weren't for Henry, Jack, Darius, and the sheer force of his anger, Joe wouldn't have made it. His stomach had started cramping from nerves in the later afternoon.

He had wanted to call Cassiel and tell her that he was bailing. But then that soft, snowflake touch of Tarika's hand on his face had happened again, and he knew he couldn't back out. Wouldn't.

He was going to choose to do this thing, for Tarika, for Cassiel, and maybe even for himself. Henry was right: it was time he started living again.

So tonight was the night, and dammit, he was going to get this thing done.

The whole group had met pretty late the night before at Sub Rosa, filling each other in on the arson, the ghosts, and plans for magic.

Through it all, Joe could feel Tarika. At one point, Cassie had given him a look. When he'd asked what it was about, she smiled and said, *"That thing you're feeling? It's real. She's right here."*

Joe was shocked Cassie could sense that, and wasn't sure if that made him feel better or worse that Tarika was still not at rest, wherever she was. But it made him more determined.

After huge arguments about needing more time, they'd all finally determined that the Christmas Eve party at the museum was the ticket. It was the only event Carter had scheduled until March.

No one was willing to wait that long. So they pushed through.

Luckily, folks had Christmas Eve day off from work. The sudden change of plans had pissed some people's family members off, but they'd been able to plan all day, pacing and plotting in Raquel's living room, with Zion filling in on coffee and tea duty.

"You ready, bro?" Henry asked, standing next to Joe's shoulder again.

"I think so. Most of this is on Darius, though." Joe jerked his chin at the tall man striding toward them, practically gleaming in the lights from the street and the closed shops. He'd gone home to take a shower and prepare himself.

They'd met until five o'clock, when Raquel had finally called a halt.

"Go home, rest, eat. Kiss your families. We all need to be as fresh as possible tonight, and that's only a few hours away."

"You sound as if we're heading to our deaths, Raquel," Tobias had quipped.

The only response she gave to that had been a flick of her fingers and a loaded look. That's when Joe started to get nervous.

But as the saying went, the only way out was through

Joe rolled his shoulders, and tugged at his wool watch cap again, bringing his attention back to the moment.

"Darius, my man."

"We good?" Darius buttoned up the top button of his wool coat against the cold.

They'd decided that Darius should dress up, like a moneyed man. He looked the part. Leather gloves. Long, navy wool coat. Polished shoes.

Except for the coat, which Joe envied, he was glad he didn't have to dress up. He was thankful for his long underwear, thick pants, and the watch cap.

"News," Henry said.

Sure enough, a camera person had just crawled out of the white news van on the opposite corner. And two other people walked up and staked out the side of the museum steps. One had a microphone; the other, a fancy camera.

The first limousine pulled up, disgorging a woman with shimmering blond hair and a red beaded dress. All she had on other than that was a pair of black, red-soled pumps and a black velvet wrap.

"That woman has to be freezing!" Joe muttered.

"She's got money to keep her warm," Henry replied.

A dark-haired white man in a tuxedo followed her out of the car.

The driver nodded at the man, thunked the door shut, then got back in the car and drove off just as two town cars and another limousine arrived.

Two more people who looked like reporters showed up, and the television reporter, a Latino man in his own long wool coat, nodded to the cameraman, who turned on his lights.

"Show time," Henry said.

"I'd better get into position," Darius said.

"We're right here, man. I've got your back," Joe said. He watched Darius walk away, almost wishing it was him who got to avenge Tarika. But he knew it had to be her brother, the one who'd obsessed over her case for months, on his own, going slowly crazy, until more help arrived in the form of an injured former boyfriend in a crowded, noisy bar.

"Let's get you closer," Henry said, "in case we got to move fast."

Joe nodded, and sent a quick thought to Cassiel. He hoped she was okay, and that the coven came through.

He felt the connection they had, like a tugging just

beneath his breastbone, and that gave him some assurance that whatever weird magic stuff Raquel and Cassie's coven was up to was actually going to have an effect here, on this sidewalk in front of the museum.

Listen to him. He might as well have turned into his dead grandmother, thinking about magic and spirits on the wind.

A light touch brushed his cheek. "You there, Tarika?" he whispered.

He felt the distinct sensation of his favorite pair of lips upon his own.

He gasped a little, then looked up.

It had started to snow.

31

CASSIEL

Cassie was out in Raquel's backyard, staring up the sky still covered in clouds. She wouldn't have been able to see the moon in any case.

Tonight, the moon was dark.

Working with the coven, Cassiel was slowly learning to appreciate the dark moon again. She used to fear it. It was often the worst part of the month. The time when the ghosts felt particularly strong.

The temperature had dropped again. Cassie had a wool hat on, and thick scarf wrapped around her neck and face, exposing only her nose and eyes.

Her gloved hands held a mug of peppermint tea. She sipped it more for comfort than anything, though it would hopefully keep her stomach settled during the work ahead.

She smelled the snow right before the soft flakes kissed her face. It was so strange for a girl from Tennessee to be sitting in a garden in Portland, Oregon, in the first soft fall of snow.

Sitting and waiting for a battle to begin. A battle that it felt like they just might win. She never felt as if there were any way to win back home in Tennessee. It never seemed as if she actually helped those poor ghosts.

Unlike the work she did with the police, and with ghosts who were lost and bewildered, or reliving the moment of their death over and over again, this ghost had a purpose. Tarika knew exactly what she wanted and seemed happy enough now that people were paying attention.

Those other ghosts? There had never been much sense to their deaths, so even with the few cases that actually got solved, there was never resolution.

There was only ever a sense of yawning need. Tarika, though? Her life's work stood a pretty good chance of being finished tonight.

Unless something major went wrong.

It was Christmas Eve, and Carter Industries was throwing a huge party. Supposedly it was a benefit for a local homeless shelter, though Lucy had scoffed that if he donated more than five percent of the ticket price, she'd give up painting houses and devote all of her energy to serving the poor.

Cassie felt a little nervous still, but also, she felt stronger and more certain than she had in years.

"You here, Tarika?" She felt a cool sweep across a small patch of the exposed skin on her face, then a slight squeeze of her right shoulder. "You're going to have to guide me in this. Okay?"

Which was another difference. The ghosts Cassiel had dealt with in the past had looked to her for everything. Tarika, the reporter, had autonomy. She had led them where she wanted them to go. She led Joe and Darius, for sure, enabling them to make the necessary connections and ferret out things that had been missed before.

And she was going to show Cassiel and the Arrow and

Crescent Coven the way to do this magic. Cassiel just knew it.

A sense of certainty settled over her. She felt the power of her namesake, the angel, and knew that yes, this was the work she had been born for. In some translations, Cassiel meant "speed of God" but in others, it meant "God is my anger."

Well, she'd spent years feeling angry at the burden of her gift. She'd used her speed to run away. But now, she was ready and willing to use anger to fuel the work that needed to be done. Anger wasn't a block or a way to avoid her psychic gifts anymore. Anger was the fuel that bolstered her abilities and supported the work.

She felt as if she should be carrying a fiery sword or something. It was nice to feel this powerful for a change.

The coven was gathering in Raquel's attic again. She knew that Joe, Darius, and Henry were outside the glitzy event downtown, ready and waiting to move.

Joe and Darius had put a ton of time into research. They had come up with enough events connecting Carter to shady events, and multiple fires, and also showed how Dixon had consistently published puff pieces on the man.

They hadn't found proof that Dixon had actively stopped publication, and the only admission that he'd had anything to do with Tarika's death was the look of guilt that crossed his face when Joe had barged into his office, slinging accusations.

Cassie felt in her bones, though, that he and Carter would both be unmasked tonight.

They were going to turn the Tower indeed. Instead of Carter's buildings falling, it was going to be the man himself, and Dixon, too. And by the Goddess, she was going to be the fire that burned that building to the ground this time.

She heard a door open behind her.

"Cassiel?" Raquel's voice carried in the night. "It's time. You ready?"

"Yes," Cassiel said. And she was. She walked up the back porch steps and carried her tea mug into the brightly lit kitchen. It smelled like lamb stew and spiced wine. That was for the feast after ritual. No matter how things went, the coven would need the sustenance and warmth.

She sent a swift thought out to Joe, and felt him respond in kind. That made her smile. That kind of connection was new, too. She'd never had that with a man before.

She was going to need that connection to do the magic tonight. The whole coven was counting on it.

Cassiel followed Raquel up the stairs to the attic, Cassie unbuttoning her coat and unwinding the long scarf as they went. She slicked the wool hat from her head and shoved it into a coat pocket before shucking out of the coat and draping it over the banister on the landing.

As soon as Raquel opened the attic door, Cassie felt the buzz of energy and tasted a hint of electricity, as though lightning had struck.

As usual, beeswax candles lit the canted walls of the attic room and every single covener sat on a bright cushion in a circle. There was one space open for Raquel. No space in the circle for Cassiel.

Her place was on the quilt laid out in the middle of the circle, where the altar would usually be.

Cassie took in a deep breath and rocked back and forth on her heels and the balls of her feet a couple of times. She rotated her head on her neck, rolled her shoulders, and flicked her fingers, shaking out her hands.

"Ready?" Brenda asked from the across the room, candlelight playing across her brown hair put up in its usual messy bun.

Cassie took a moment to look around the circle. Moss, wearing a plain black T-shirt for once. Face serious. Alejandro. Lucy. Selene. Tempest. Tobias with his wispy goatee. Everyone was in black tonight.

"We need to be as incognito as possible. And we need to link together. We also need to link to the power of the dark moon. So in favor of setting up a strong resonance for the working, we should all wear black." That was Raquel's idea. She was right. Cassiel could feel the energy rising. She felt the slight hum of the circle they had cast while she was centering herself outside.

She murmured a quick prayer to Diana, the patron Goddess of their coven, and also to Cassiel the angel.

Sparing another quick thought for Tarika, she sank down onto the quilt, checked in on her emotional connection with Joe, and began the process that would enable her to astral travel.

32

JOE

Darius moved swiftly toward the steps and the clump of newscasters. Joe hoped the coven was on point with whatever the heck spooky stuff they had planned.

The crowd in front of the museum had grown into a well-heeled throng, all heading toward the big glass doors, where warmth, champagne, and thousand dollar hors d'oeuvres awaited them.

Despite his wool socks, long underwear, and gloves, Joe's wrist and ankle ached from the cold. He hoped this was all over soon.

He also hoped the fire inspector would be able to pin something on Dixon and Carter. That would only help the case as it went on.

Tonight wasn't about absolute proof. Tonight was about asking the right questions. Raising suspicion. Making a stink so bad that the city wouldn't want to ignore it.

Reporters were cutthroat, but they also hated it when one of their own was threatened. For Tarika to have been murdered?—and Joe was now convinced she was—well, let's just say he hoped the situation would become a pitched battle. And soon.

Darius was in position.

"You ready for this, bro?" Henry asked.

"Yes. Absolutely." Joe felt a certainty about all of this that he hadn't felt since he and Tarika first fell in love. He might never become a crusader like she was, but dammit, he sure as hell could do his best to make things right.

Jack showed up then, huffing a little. "I had to park ten blocks away. The limousines took up all the empty spots."

"You coulda just paid for a spot, man," Henry replied, an amused smirk on his face. "You'd think you were an accountant instead of a game designer."

Jack just waved his hand as if to brush Henry aside. "What's happening? Anything yet?"

"We're stilling waiting for Carter to show," Joe replied. He'd gone still inside. Waiting. He could sense Cassie overhead somewhere, which was a little weird, but felt good all the same. *"Hope you don't mind, babe,"* he thought. He felt a hand squeeze his shoulder and another brush along his cheek.

The snow had begun to fall in earnest. The fancy people were rushing up the steps as quickly as possible.

The television news crew started shut down. Tired of waiting in the cold. The camera shut off the lights. The change in lighting caused one of the wealthy woman to trip in her heels. Her date caught her right before she hit the steps, righting her again and, arm around her, hurried toward the doorman at the top of the steps.

A buzzing started from the by now freezing newspeople as a black town car arrived.

"Got to be Carter," Henry said.

"I'm getting closer." Joe caned his way forward, wincing

with every step. His whole body hurt by now, from trying not to shiver, from the ache in his bones, and from the tension of it all.

He didn't care. But he also couldn't wait anymore.

"Carter!" he yelled into the gathering white swirl.

"What are you doing, man?" Henry said, right behind him.

Carter's blond head snapped toward the noise. Darius stepped up and put a hand on the man's arm. Joe could see him speaking, but Carter was distracted, wondering who had shouted his name. Good. Throw him off balance.

Cameras started clicking. Flashes going off. The news camera started up again, flooding the scene with light, and the reporter hurried back.

Joe heard the buzz of voices as he approached, and heard Darius speaking, loudly and clearly.

"Mr. Carter," Darius was saying, "are you the owner of Carter Industries, Homes Unlimited, Strategic Planning, and Advance Development?"

Joe was close enough to see a dark flush creeping up from Carter's collar. Good.

The man sputtered. "I have no idea who you are, but I've got guests to attend to!"

"Mr. Carter, is it true that each one of these companies that you own has suffered a major fire right before their developments were completed?"

Oh. Darius was good under pressure. Man. The reporters were scribbling madly, or talking into handheld recorders. The big news camera filmed the whole scene.

The snow was falling thick and fast. Joe didn't care anymore. It was as if Tarika was swirling in the air around him. Cassiel, too. He felt both women, working their hardest to pull this shit off.

"Carter!" he yelled again, almost on top of the crowd.

Carter's head whipped around again. Joe knew he could see him this time, a skinny, pale brown man in workman's clothing, hobbling toward him like a maniac, wool cap on his head.

"Mr. Carter! Is it true you and Greg Dixon had investigative journalist Tarika Henderson killed to keep her from breaking this story?"

The whole crowd turned toward Joe, the camera floodlight practically blinding him.

He squinted through the light and the falling snow, and kept moving eyes trained on Carter, but angling toward Darius, so they could stand as a united front.

The pain in his ankle spiked. Joe hissed, but kept moving.

One step at a time, Joe. One step at a time.

"Carter!" he shouted again. "Are you going to answer my question?"

33

CASSIEL

The astral plane was still not a place Cassiel was used to. She shouldn't have been the one doing this, but both Brenda and Raquel had insisted. She was the one most closely tied to the situation—and to Joe—so she would have the clearest connection, they said.

And the greatest effect.

She tried to acclimate herself to floating so far outside her physical body, but the sense of vertigo hadn't yet abated. Cassie felt a dim sense of her physical body. There was a queasiness and the aching at the back of her neck that she got when a fever was coming on.

She hoped that was just from the fact that her spirit had lifted itself out and was floating further from the physical than she'd ever been before. Cassiel didn't want to get sick. Not on top of everything else going on.

"Focus, Cassie," she told herself, and tuned back in to the space around her, a floating pearly gray and lavender mist that felt like a cavernous hall of some sort.

Cassiel took a huge breath in, not knowing whether her physical body would breathe that deeply too. But it was what she was used to when trying to do any sort of magical operation, so she was going to stick with what she knew, astral body or not.

Cassiel saw the threads that Tobias, Brenda, and Tempest were spooling out from down below and caught ahold of them. Those three were the strongest empaths in the coven, and had tapped into both Carter and Dixon, throwing their signatures to Cassie. Tempest had also tuned in on two other developers, including the one that owned the management company for Cassiel's building.

The threads were more like slender ropes of pulsing energy. A shade of deep royal blue. A sickly, noxious green. And a washed-out tan. Some slimmer threads wound themselves around the other three.

She assumed two of the skeins were Carter and Dixon, and wondered who the third influential party would turn out to be. There were several options Darius and Joe had uncovered, including the mayor, but nothing seemed concrete.

The cords pulsed with anger. The anger of powerful men feeling cheated, she supposed. Forced into dealings that were beneath them.

Angry at being forced to provide low income housing instead of filling the city with homes and apartments at the rising market rate. Pissed that they had to deal with a city council when not all the members were easily bribed. Many likely were, but these days, it seemed that many was not enough.

Corruption and graft just weren't what they used to be.

Cassiel needed all of this information to get into the men. To fade beneath their skin. To turn the Tower and pull back the veil.

She knew that Alejandro was working with Carter's logo,

that golden wagon wheel that represented his company name. She hoped that would help key her in as well.

As soon as the thought passed through her head, she saw a distant shape, hovering above her on the astral plane. From this distance, it looked like a white oval. She zoomed closer in, and saw that the thing kept shifting, from a white mask, to a ring of fire, to a flock of pigeons racing toward the sky.

Beneath all of these was a purple veil, surrounding an object.

Cassie forced herself to move closer still, and to soften and sharpen her psychic eyes to more clearly see. And there it was. An image so clear she couldn't believe she'd never seen it before.

At the heart of the shifting visage was a bloodred ruby, the size of her fist.

A large golden wheel rotated slowly around it.

She paused for a moment, feeling the energy of the threads in her hands and trying to tune into the chunk of raw, unpolished ruby. What was it?

Patterns on the astral represented patterns on earth, in physical space and time.

Cassie closed her astral eyes, even though she knew that didn't make any sense. She always sensed things better with her eyes closed, another thing Brenda wanted her to work on.

There. The wagon wheel carried resonances of all the threads, but was mostly one. The blue. Because of the color of his company signs, Cassie assumed that was Carter. The blue wove its way through the edges of the wheel, coloring it and causing variegated shadows on the spokes.

The tan is Dixon, a voice whispered in her inner ear. Tarika. Good. That connection was working, at least. She hoped her connection to Joe was clear as well. She couldn't sense him. She just had to hope that every time she sent a thought his way, he caught it. Or hoped Tarika could act as an intermediary somehow.

Okay. How about the green, and the other, thinner cords? Probably other developers or interests. Either the coven was working on it, or they'd get that information later.

Cassie just hoped knowing who two of the main sources of power that were compromising the city were would be enough for now.

And that a barely trained, half-sick-with-astral-vertigo witch would have enough skill to take them down.

Cassiel took another breath, tightened her grip on the threads, and moved toward the shifting images that swirled around that ruby heart.

The ruby heart. Bounded by the golden wheel. It must be the heart of the city. That felt right to her. The ruby flared. She sent an image of it along to Joe.

Reaching past the mask, the wheel, the birds...her fingertips touched the pulsing purple veil.

It felt like ice, singeing the edges of her skin. Her hand jerked back on its own.

"Come on, Cassiel," she said through clenched teeth, shaking out her hand. Her fingers looked fine. "This isn't your physical body. You can do this."

She wasn't one-hundred-percent certain that was true, either part of the statement. If the spiritual affected the physical, maybe this would, too. And whether or not she could do this?

Well, she'd find out any second now.

"What the hell are you two talking about? I don't have time for this shit."

The civilized mask was starting to slip. *Good job, Cassiel,* Joe thought. The space beneath his breastbone where he felt connected to her was the only part of him that was warm.

Whatever work she and the coven was doing, it was working. Carter was not a man who let much slip, ever. Joe would bet on it. Even standing in falling snow, head uncovered, in nothing but a tuxedo with a sober burgundy waistcoat, the man looked perfect.

Not a shining hair out of place.

"Who are you?" a reporter called out.

Darius straightened, standing even taller than he had been before, snow dusting the shoulders of his dark wool coat. The snow melted on the close-cut cap of his hair. It was starting to run down his face. Even with all that, he looked handsome as could be, perfect for television. A person would never know that he was also the haunted man Joe had left in his apartment with its string-covered walls.

"My name is Darius Henderson. I am the brother of slain journalist Tarika Henderson. We are calling on authorities to re-open the case of her alleged suicide because new facts have come to light implicating Mr. Carter in her death, along with Mr. Dixon of the *Mount Tabor Monthly*."

In for a damn penny, Darius. Good job. If they got sued, they got sued. The press generated by a slander lawsuit would be worth whatever time and money it cost.

And Joe was sure there was a lawyer somewhere in town who wanted Carter's skin, and might be happy to take on a pro-bono case.

"You're full of shit!" Carter spat out. "I have no idea what you're talking about. I barely even know Greg Dixon."

Well, that wasn't true. Joe had seen a photograph to prove it. Happy cronies, golfing. Carter. Dixon. And the mayor...

"We'll be happy to supply the press with our findings, which are considerable," Darius continued, speaking directly to the reporters now.

Carter didn't like being ignored. He shoved Darius backward, knocking him into a photographer on the step behind. Darius recovered, but the photographer fell with a hard smack.

"Mr. Carter! Sir!" His driver rushed up the steps. Joe wasn't sure if he was going to try to get Carter away, or stop him from striking anyone else.

Joe shoved himself forward, two more steps. Almost there. He felt a slight pressure on his shoulder: Tarika's hand, steadying him.

"Carter!" Joe yelled. "Tarika Henderson was working on a story about a series of fires on large construction sites throughout Washington, Oregon, and Idaho. We have proof that all these fires generated on building sites of companies and holdings that you own."

The television cameraman stepped closer and the reporter shoved a microphone in Carter's face.

"Any comment on these allegations, Mr. Carter?" she asked. Her rose-red lips glowed in the light and her eyes looked like a predator's in the middle of her beautiful, dark brown face.

"Fuck all of you!" Carter screamed, trying to push his way through the small throng. "Let me out of here!"

Oh yeah. The mask was ripped all the way off now.

The driver shoved an arm through, trying to pull Carter out. Reporters closed around him, as did a small group of onlookers, including a few people from the houseless encampment two blocks over, dressed in lumpy layers against the freeze.

Help me out, Tarika. Cassiel. We're not quite there yet.

A thought glimmered at the edges of his mind. He felt a pulse in his solar plexus. Then his phone buzzed in his pocket.

Fumbling it out of his coat, he read:

DARIUS. CITY.

Right. There was something...

"Darius." Joe was finally next to Tarika's brother, who was breathing hard, vapor exiting his mouth into the freezing night. He looked calm, otherwise. As though all of the crazed energy he'd been living with had fled.

"Yeah, man."

"There's one other piece of information you had...I'm not quite there with it. Something about city money."

"I got you, man."

Joe hoped he did. This seemed a little too easy so far, as though everything was going according to plan.

Whipping his head around, his eyes search the small crowd. He saw Henry and Jack, who both gave him a thumbs-up.

Then he saw someone at the edges, another dude in fancy clothes. Head bent, he was speaking rapidly into his phone.

Then Joe heard sirens.

35

CASSIEL

The symbols flipped faster and faster around Cassie as her right hand hit the icy veil again. Grimacing against the shocking pain of the cold, she turned her fingers into claws and gripped the gauzy veil, beginning to lift it from the pulsing red stone.

The icy veil shredded at her touch, as though nothing was holding it together anymore.

"Damn!" She shook her hand out again and watched the pieces of the astral veil disintegrate before her eyes.

Literally, it dis-integrated, shred by shred, until nothing was left. The white mask exploded, and the ring of fire rolled outward, scattering the image of the pigeons in its wake.

Cassie resisted the urge to duck. The shattering symbols didn't seem able to touch her, but it was hard to not flinch all the same.

She reached, wrapping her right hand around the ruby chunk. Where the veil had been cold, the ruby was warm, almost hot, as though lit with an internal fire. The fire in the hearts of the almost six hundred thousand people who lived in Portland. All of their hope, creativity, and love.

She caught a whiff of mingled kerosene and gasoline, and a vision of fire filled her head. The wheel was on fire.

A great cracking sound split the astral plane.

"The Tower..." she murmured, and held on to the ruby, even as flames surrounded her, rising from the wheel battering at her body, and the scent and taste of gasoline filled her mouth and nose. Clinging to the ropes of energy in her left hand, she tried to *send* to the rest of the coven, hoping they could see and feel what she was sensing.

She sent an extra pulse to Joe.

"I. Need. Help."

Her teeth ground against each other and Cassie began to shake, trembling with the shock and effort of it all.

She was afraid to let go, but didn't know how much longer she could hold on.

A pulse came through the ropy threads in her left hand, and with the pulse, information entered her body. Not so much information, as awareness.

The coven had caught a pattern and were trying to send it back to her. There was a key piece of information they didn't have before. Someone in the coven must have gotten it tonight.

Right. Alejandro. Something about the sigils and symbols. He'd figured something out. That wheel symbol connected to something important.

In her mind's eye, she saw the green flow of binary computer code, overlaid with other symbols. That was all Alejandro's language though. Not hers.

"I need something else, guys. Come on! I'm about to lose it here!"

Open. Just that one word. Repeated again. *Open.*

Cassiel heaved in a great breath, opened her eyes wide, and looked down.

Then her whole being relaxed.

Her hands dropped the ruby and the cords, and she floated upward, hands and arms and legs spread wide, like a parachuter plummeting to the ground, only she plummeted *up*, looking down, down, down.

Down onto the earth. Down onto the city. Down onto the spread of connection from city to town to forest to city again.

And she Saw it then. She Saw all the places the fires had burned, were burning, would burn.

She saw the toxic rivers flowing in between them. She saw the webbing of distraction, misdirection, and of lies.

Three men were at the heart of it. Dixon. Carter. And the mayor of Portland himself.

"Mayor Johnny Patterson. Gotcha." She tried to send that information outward, in a burst, through her connections to Tarika and Joe, not sure if or how they would get it. Only hoping that everything she'd been sending all along had gotten through.

Joe and Darius needed this information. It was the missing key. Cassiel was certain of it now.

Pressure built inside her from the effort and she felt a tugging at her solar plexus. She'd been away from her body too long.

"Oh shit," she said.

Everything went black.

36

JOE

S irens dopplered toward the museum, and the glittering patrons—who should have been enjoying a string quartet and their very expensive party—crowded just inside the big glass doors, peering out into the night.

Red, blue, and white lights flashed across the crowd on the steps, setting the snow flurries dancing with color.

This could be good, or could be bad. Depended on how deep the corruption went.

"Need to get out of here, bro?" Henry asked. He and Jack flanked Joe now, ready to help him away if need be.

"I'm already on film, and even with your help, I can't move quickly enough to evade the cops. Besides, I'm not abandoning Darius here."

The men all looked at Darius. He had a strange smile on his face and continued to talk with the reporters, calmly, as though a white man wasn't practically spitting and clawing at his face. Two men were trying, with partial success, to hold Carter back.

The man was seriously melting down. Not Darius, though. It was as though he had channeled all the anguish and worry of the past months into a solid determination that he was right, and going to see it through.

Joe knew that feeling. It felt like liberation.

Anything else, Cassiel? Tarika?

No question about it now, he was turning into his grandmother for sure. Standing in a crowd, listening for voices on the wind.

The police were coming up the steps now, trying to figure out what was going on, and who, if anyone, they should arrest.

In any other circumstances, it would have been clear that the big man being physically restrained by two others was the culprit. But when that man was also clearly rich and white, it sowed confusion.

And somehow Joe was pretty certain they knew exactly who Carter was.

The phone buzzed in his pocket again.

MAYOR.

Joe shook his head, and almost crowed with laughter, heady with the strangeness of it all. This was like being drunk on the best beer brewed by the best microbrewery in Portland.

Of course. Of course it was the mayor. That photograph above Dixon's desk. And how else had Carter gotten all these deals through?

The police moved through the clumps of people, asking what was going on.

Might as well go for it, confirmation or not. Joe raised his voice. "I'd like to announce that we have more information than we've mentioned so far. Along with Carter, and Dixon, this information also implicates Mayor Patterson himself."

The police stopped in their tracks, heads swiveling toward Joe.

Darius's eyes widened briefly before he smiled again. He gave Joe the "okay" sign. Huh. That was interesting.

"These are very serious allegations," said one of the newspaper reporters. "Do you have actual proof to back it up?"

Darius pulled something from the pocket of his long, navy coat, and held it aloft.

"What is it?"

"This, my friends, is a thumb drive filled with every scrap of information Tarika Henderson gathered for her exposé. She was almost ready to release the story before she was taken from us." Darius looked around, catching the eyes of several of the reporters gathered there. Then he spoke into the television camera. "My sister only needed another item or two that I'm sure you fine people could ferret out in no time, given all the footwork she already did for you all. The information on this thumb drive clearly implicates all three men."

Holy shit. Darius found one of Tarika's thumb drives? How in the world? He must have stayed up half the night, searching. Through what? Her boxes? Hadn't they gone through all her stuff after she died?

The reporters all seemed to be talking at once, shouting questions, talking to each other. Some of the people inside the museum spilled out, gaping. Joe wanted to raise his cane in the air in victory. Only the slippery concrete and his bad ankle kept him from it. Jack slapped Henry on the back.

"Hoohoo! This is wild!" Jack said.

Carter punched Darius in the face. Darius rocked backwards again, taking down two reporters as he went.

The police moved quickly, grabbing Carter's hands and he flailed and spat, face red, hair finally out of place.

"You don't know what you're talking about. I've done

more for this city than anyone! So has Patterson! I'm going to sue every last one of you!"

His head whipped toward the TV camera.

"You, too! If you run this tape, I'm suing the pants of your station! You'll never recover!"

"Mr. Carter. Mr. Carter. Let's go..." one of the cops said.

"Get your hands off of me! Do you know who I am?" He jerked his arm, dragging the cop with him.

The cop scowled and reached for his cuffs.

"Yes sir. I know exactly who you are."

Joe heard the cuffs against Carter's wrists. *Smack. Smack.*

Another cop appeared next to Joe. When had more police arrived? "We'll need to talk with you, sir. If you don't mind making a quick statement over in the squad car, we can get out of this snow. We'll need a more complete statement later."

"After Christmas?" Joe asked. He might as well push his luck, right? Tonight had already been unbelievable.

"No promises, but probably."

Henry and Jack were helping Darius up. One of the reporters tried to fashion the dry snow into an improvised ice pack for Darius's already swelling cheek.

"Damn, Darius, you okay?" Joe called out.

"I'm great, man. Just great." He was smiling.

Joe smiled back.

"Sir?" the cop said.

"Sorry. We gotta go slow. I can't move too fast with this cane."

37

CASSIEL

Cassiel had her feet curled onto Raquel's overstuffed red couch, with a rust-colored soft throw blanket tucked around her legs and a steaming cup of hot chocolate in her hands. She'd pulled the sleeves of her green sweater down around her hands.

Tobias had laid a fire before heading into the kitchen.

"That'll keep you warm," he said. What a good guy he was.

The whole coven had been so great to her, she didn't even mind not having the money to go to Tennessee for Christmas.

The sounds of laughter came from the kitchen, along with the scent of baking sweet potatoes and ham. The rest of the coven was in there, along with Henry, Jack, and Darius. They were just waiting for Joe, so they could debrief and answer some of the last few questions running through everyone's heads.

It was two days after Christmas and had been snowing off and on ever since the night of the big magic. Cassie couldn't seem to keep warm.

"We shouldn't have let you stay out so long," Brenda had said.

But Cassie knew they had to. First off, it wasn't clear that Tarika could have done the work she needed without Cassiel up on the astral, manipulating the æthers. And from everything the coven had found out since, there was no way Carter's mask would have cracked without the work the coven and Cassie had done.

And if Cassie didn't have the connection she did with Tarika and Joe? None of it would have worked, either. It was good, but strange, to have a network like that. To not have to go it alone.

Carter was a smooth, slick operator. No one had been able to pin any dirt on him for years. Not until Tarika started nosing around.

All the news wasn't out yet, but it was looking like Darius and Joe's suppositions were correct. Carter had used Dixon to kill Tarika. And Mayor Patterson had likely been cutting deals with Carter for years.

Cassie sipped her chocolate and stared up at the painting of the Sun tarot card above the mantel. This one had a black child that looked a lot like Zion, running, arms outstretched, the whole sky lit up with orange and yellow rays behind his head.

It felt like a good omen, that painting, even though Cassiel knew Raquel had commissioned it two years before. It felt like the time of The Tower was passing. Cassie felt that in her bones.

She just didn't know what this new phase was going to look like. She hoped she had what it took to open to whatever it was.

Where was Joe? Cassiel hadn't seen him in days. She found that she missed his shy smile. The part of her that had been thinking something might be happening between them wasn't sure anymore.

She felt so raw, vulnerable. Still a little shaky. She'd missed Christmas entirely, having slept most of the day curled up in a ball on her bed.

A knock came at the front door, and then it opened, letting in a rush of cold before it snicked closed again.

And there he was, swiping a wool cap from his head with his left hand. He still had a cane in his right, but his left arm wasn't in a sling anymore.

"Hey there." He smiled at her, warm and good. Cassiel couldn't help but smile back. There was something different about him. His eyes held hers in a steady gaze. As if he wasn't afraid of her anymore. Or whatever it was that made him so nervous all the time.

Shucking out of his heavy work coat, he piled it on top of the already overfull coat tree in the entryway, then came and sat down next to her on the couch.

"How are you doing?" he asked. "I tried calling, but..."

"Oh. Yeah. My phone battery died and I didn't realize it. Sorry. I've been pretty out of it the past few days."

He just nodded, eyes not leaving her face.

"I checked in with Raquel when I hadn't heard from you. She told me you were in a bad way, but that the coven had you well covered in the chicken soup department."

That startled a soft laugh out of her. "Yeah. Convincing them to leave me alone so I could sleep took some doing."

She shivered, and went to set the hot chocolate mug down so she could hike the rust throw further up.

"Let me." Joe reached out, and with two gentle hands, tucked the blanket more firmly around her. His face was inches from her own.

Cassie swallowed.

He looked into her eyes again, then softly squeezed her shoulder before sitting back.

"You're not in a sling anymore."

Joe looked down at his arms. "Yeah. I went to the doctor yesterday. She said I was fine. It still aches a bit, but she said as long as I'm careful to not bash it against something, I'm okay. I still need another week or so off work, though. Don't want to put too much pressure on the joint."

She sipped her hot chocolate, letting the cinnamon and cocoa do its work. She didn't know what to say.

"You still haven't answered my question, Cassiel. How are you?"

"I'm...not great, to be honest. That took a lot out of me." She stared at the white and pale brown bubbles on the surface of chocolate for a moment, still wishing the warmth would fill her all the way up again. "Both Brenda and Raquel said my spirit spent too long outside my body, on the astral. It's still affecting me, I guess."

"I'd like to hear about it sometime. I mean, not just the debrief we have planned today, but what it was like for you."

"You don't think it's crazy?" she asked. "The girl who talks to ghosts and does weird stuff that most people think is just pretend?"

It was his turn to laugh this time.

"I'm the one that got injured because my dead girlfriend was trying to get a hold of me through my cell phone."

Cassiel retreated a little, burrowing back into the cushions.

Joe noticed.

"About that, Cassie..." He leaned toward her, arm thrown over the back of the couch. "I loved Tarika. I really did. I hate that she died. Was killed. But she's been dead for almost as long as we dated and..."

"And what?" she asked.

"And the work we all did on Christmas Eve? I feel good about it. Stronger. It meant something. And you were part of that. Our connection helped make it happen. And after that work? I think she's finally gone."

Cassiel nodded. "Yeah. It feels that way to me, too. She came to visit me on Christmas night, I think. To say thank you."

She looked up and saw tears glimmering in Joe's eyes.

"I dreamed about her that night, too. She looked happy. Like she used to. We were walking next to the Willamette. She gave me one last hug, told me to thank you, and then just...faded. I'm glad she got to tell you herself."

Cassie set her mug onto the coffee table and reached for his hand.

"I'm glad, too."

38

JOE

J oe always felt at home at Raquel's, which was good, because here he was, finally alone with Cassiel. Being in a familiar, comfortable environment always helped his social anxiety.

But looking at Cassiel, he found that for the first time with her, he didn't feel anxious at all. Maybe whatever they'd done on Christmas Eve had changed him, or maybe it was that Cassiel looked less confident than usual herself, and it was throwing off his usual pattern.

He still felt that connection with her, warming up the space at the bottom of his sternum. He thought she felt it, too.

Her face was thinner, and there were definite shadows around her eyes. She looked only half there to him. As though part of her was floating off somewhere.

Joe hoped Cassiel came all the way back, because she also still looked absolutely beautiful, sitting across from him, one pale hand curled around his.

He liked that. A lot.

Fire crackled at the hearth, sparking and snapping. It

felt good after being out on the snow-covered ground. Henry had cleared the sidewalks, at least, which was why he'd finally felt comfortable letting Joe walk over on his own.

"It's literally *next door*," Joe had said.

"Yeah, and you're literally *walking with a cane*, bro," Henry had replied.

Brothers. Gotta love them.

Tarika was finally laid to rest. Oh, it would take time for the whole story to come out, and maybe everyone wouldn't be convicted in the long run. Payoffs were still a thing, and wealthy people could hire lawyers to work the system up and down until they got off with a fine, or completely free.

Darius was giving interview after interview, and good for him. Let him. Joe had no interest in being in the public eye.

They were all here today to celebrate and debrief. And to blow off some steam. God knew, Joe needed it.

Looking at this woman on the couch with him, red hair tumbled around her pale face, gray eyes too big for the moment, he wanted nothing more than to help Cassie find her way back home again.

Speaking of homes...

He gently squeezed her hand.

"I talked with Henry again. Our offer still stands. If you still need a place to live after all of this, we've got an extra room. We'd be happy for you to stay as long as you want."

She looked at him, startled.

"I...the Tenants Union says the new information you and Darius uncovered might give us all a stronger case to keep our homes. That it's a sign of citywide corruption. But they're also not sure it will happen quickly enough. At least not for me. But for now, I'm going to stay and fight. I'm going to refuse to pay the rent increase and see what happens."

"Wow! That's great, Cassiel! Let me know if you need backup."

The sounds from the kitchen were increasing. There was some serious hilarity going on in there, and the food smelled great.

She took a deep breath in and drew her hand away, tilting her head down until her hair fell forward to obscure her face. She stayed that way for a moment, before finally sitting back on the couch and tugging the rust-colored blanket back around her.

Joe had to stop himself from helping her again.

She looked up, face looking as though she'd come to some sort of decision.

"So," she said, "you actually still want to go on that real date? I promise not to rush off, ready to throw up next time."

"Hah! Yeah. Yes. I do."

Good. She was seeming more like herself again. At least, more like the woman he'd met in Raquel's café.

The sound of plates and bowls getting stacked on kitchen counters filtered through the door. Joe could hear Raquel's son, Zion. He was all excited about something or other.

"You know what, though?"

"What?" Joe replied.

"I think we should get that awkward first kiss out of the way."

Joe's heart stopped in his chest for an instant, and he sucked in a breath.

Then he leaned toward her, taking in his favorite scents of pine trees, damp rich soil, and rain.

"Cassiel, has anyone ever told you that you smell just like a forest?"

"No."

He scooted closer on the couch. "Well, you do."

Then they each put a hand on the back of the other's necks, and drew their faces all the way toward each other.

Their lips touched, and held, just for a moment.

Joe buried his hands in that red fall of hair and kissed Cassiel with everything he had.

And she kissed him right back.

It was delicious.

Reviews can make or break a book's success.
If you enjoyed this book, please consider telling a friend, or
leaving a short review at your favorite booksellers or on
GoodReads.
Many thanks!

Pick up the next book in series: By Flame

Click for a free short story collection, or visit thorncoyle.com.

READ AN EXCERPT OF BY FLAME, THE
WITCHES OF PORTLAND, BOOK TWO

AVAILABLE MID-MAY, 2018

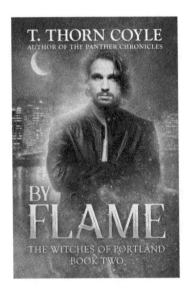

BY FLAME: CHAPTER ONE

Tobias had been fighting his demons since childhood. Fighting the voices that told him he wasn't good enough, and would never fit in. That he was stupid. Lacked ambition. Cried like a girl. And then, as he grew older, fighting the opinions that he was wasting his life.

The demons sounded an awful lot like his father.

Tobias stared out the window, past the shaking needles of the towering pine, at the rain-slicked street and cars shushing by. The morning's soft rainfall had increased, smacking harder on the window of the office space he rented in a large, three-story Craftsman. He turned from the window.

The office was small, but suited his needs. Tobias had settled in here six months ago, and it was finally starting to feel like home. He looked around his cozy space, at his favorite chair, dark brown, stuffed just right, and comfortable. A client chair, a wingback in deep blue and chocolate stripes, faced it across a small coffee table. The desk where he wrote up his notes and worked with his herbs was a long slab, a heavy oak door that he'd rescued from a sidewalk and propped up on two old filing cabinets. There were plants and jars of herbs on shelves everywhere, and seedlings under a grow lamp.

Between the herbs and the incense he burned at the office altar, the room always smelled good. Rosemary and thyme, verbena and datura, and the sharp undercut of vervain and some of the other nightshades, the herbs that grew in darkness under the light of the moon.

Usually just the scent of herbs made him want to work, but not today. Today, he felt restless, fractious. Brittle. He'd barely gotten through his meditation practice this morning, and had finally given up, deciding to just head to work, hoping that the change of scene would help.

Always awkward, often angry, Tobias stuffed his emotions down, deep inside himself, and simply got on with his life as best he could. But the emotions didn't go away. They just remained in hiding. And they still had way more control of Tobias's life than he wanted, even after an aborted attempt at therapy and after working with his coven for years.

It was getting ridiculous, and he knew it. Anyone else would say his life was perfect now. Perfect coven. Perfect home, with perfect housemates. Perfectly good herbalism practice.

"Go back to therapy, Tobias," Selene, one of his favorite coven mates, would say. "You were barely scratching the surface when you quit with Dr. Greene."

Selene was probably right. But still, Tobias didn't go. He was frightened of what he might find if he poked the shadows too often, or too hard. He had worked with Dr. Greene two years ago, when the anger at this father started choking off his ability to tune into the herbs. It had helped. His healing ability had returned, at least.

But now? The demons seemed to be dancing around him again, and he wasn't even sure why.

That's a lie, he thought.

He fingered a small sunwheel made of woven straw. A Brigid's cross. He'd been making them all week, in honor of the Goddess he was dedicated to. It was her time of year.

The little solar cross was a distraction, but no comfort. Tobias was angry again; it simmered on a low flame, deep inside his stomach. All because his father had called, all politeness and judgment. Battering him down. Subtly sneering at his life. At the fact that he had housemates, instead of a down payment on a Pearl District condo.

Reminding Tobias that in his father's mind, he was a failure, and always would be. Oh, his dad said he was okay with Tobias being gay. He was a good liberal, after all. But he'd beaten Tobias for any perceived slight or weakness.

His father insisted on using his belt on Tobias's bare skin. It was more humiliating that way. The beatings had started because of Tobias's crying, but continued even after the tears had stopped for good. Tobias still had a scar, slightly raised and pale, where his left butt cheek met his thigh. One day, after Tobias had failed a biology test, his father had reversed the belt, smacking him—just that once—with the buckle. His mother intervened that day. The only time she ever had.

Bitch. His father was a grade-A major asshole, but his mother was frankly not much better. They were both snobs. And neither of them liked him very much.

So yeah, his life was perfect to anyone looking at it from the outside. Raised rich, with every advantage, in a fancy

Eastmoreland Tudor. Reed College for his undergrad. Pre-med.

But Tobias? He doubted that perfection every day. Not only had he rejected the family wealth, he kept waiting for the moment when someone would stand up, point, and shout "Imposter!" at him, revealing him to be what he was: just a mid-twenties white guy who didn't know what the hell he was doing.

He hid it well, most of the time. He had to. People didn't want to come to an herbalist for healing if the healer was a damn mess, seething with anger and unexamined emotions.

He was brooding again, when he should be working. Turning toward his office space, he looked around, trying to decide where to even begin.

A long row of woven solar crosses lined the back of the desk, leaning up against the white wall. He set the cross in his hands down in the empty spot he'd taken it from.

He didn't doubt the power of the herbs. Never had. The plants had wisdom he would never gainsay. He just doubted *his* ability to heal, to use the herbs the way they whispered that they wanted and needed to be used.

Because he couldn't heal himself.

Couldn't heal the aching in his heart that said he'd always be alone. Couldn't heal the anger that burned so many layers down even he could forget it was there half the time. Couldn't heal the alternating disregard and active disdain he got from his parents, and the dismissal from his aunt, who had set up a trust to fund his medical school tuition, when he told her he wasn't going after all.

"I want to study herbal medicine," he told her. Aunt Lydia had scoffed and told him he was on his own. She hadn't spoken to him since. Fine with him.

Well, here he was, at twenty-seven, and his business had

just barely tipped over into the black. Like the plants in his greenhouse, it was starting to thrive. He'd even been able to open his own small practice, not attached to the naturopath's where he had worked for a couple of years when he'd finished with herbalism school. New clients kept arriving, rain or shine, to ring his bell.

These were all things that should have proven the voices were wrong. That he had a chance to grow, and to heal. That maybe, just maybe, now was the time.

Tobias sighed. This introspection would keep for another time. He really needed to get to work now.

Everyone said what a great healer he was. "You have a way with herbs," Brenda, his coven mentor, said. "It's a real gift Tobias. Don't squander it."

Well, he wasn't so sure about that. All he knew was he had to keep working.

At any rate, today was another day. He had clients to see, formulas to concoct, and emails to answer. But first, as always, Tobias started his work day with prayer.

He turned toward his altar and took a deep breath, preparing to center himself. "Every act begins with breath," Brenda had told him when he first joined Arrow and Crescent. Ever since that day, he'd tried to be more conscious about it. To make breathing itself a practice.

The altar was a small, salvaged table covered with a white cloth, with a cast-bronze Brigid's cross that came from Ireland, a bowl of water, a small dish of salt, and whatever plant he was working with in the moment arranged on top. This week, the plant was thyme.

Okay, let's get on with this. He took another breath, *snicked* a match to flame, and lit the fragrant beeswax candle. He found his center, the place of stillness deep inside of him, his guiding post, his north star. Tobias reach out with his mind and felt the elements around him: earth, fire, air, water. He dropped and opened his attention, to feel the ground beneath him, the sky above him.

Silently, he prayed to Brigid to help him in his work. To center him. To make the anger go away.

When he finished, he felt calmer; at least, enough to shove aside the emotions and get to work.

He sat at the desk and flipped open his laptop. He always checked email to see if there were last-minute notes from clients before he started in on mixing new formulas from the tinctures he'd already prepared. He got to work, surrounded by the scent of the herbs. He scrolled through, clicking past advertisements, dragging things into the trash, and then he saw the notice.

The subject line just read "Sara." Sara was one of his clients. But he didn't recognize the email the note was coming from. He clicked, and his breath caught in his throat. It felt as though his heart would stop.

Oh no, Sara, oh no.

He knew it was possible of course; Sara had been very ill. She'd been working with Western doctors for years.

Tobias had helped her manage some of the side effects of the medications she was taking, and he knew he'd helped to ease her pain. But he'd really hoped, unspoken, but infused in every tincture, that this time he could save her. He'd hoped he would come across the right combination that would strengthen Sara to fight the disease that had her in its clutches. It hadn't worked.

"Sara died peacefully in her sleep last night," the note read. "I know she loved you, and loved working with you, and would have wanted you to know. Please let us know if there were any outstanding bills; we will pay her debts for her. She gave us so much in her life; we'll do everything we can for her in her death. I'll keep you updated on services. Best wishes, Jane—Sara's sister."

Tobias closed his computer, put his head in his hands, and began to weep, softly at first, then great gusts of tears and sound, loud enough to drown out the rain.

It was the first time he had cried since he was twelve.

ACKNOWLEDGMENTS

I give thanks to the cafés of my new hometown, Portland, Oregon. All you baristas are fine human beings.

Thanks also to Leslie Claire Walker, my intrepid first reader, to Dayle Dermatis, editor extraordinaire, to Lou Harper for my covers, and to my writing buddies for getting me out of the house.

Speaking of house...thanks as always to Robert and Jonathan.

Big, grateful shout out to the members of the Sorcery Collective for spreading the word!

And last...

Thanks to all the activists and witches working your magic in the world. This series is for you.

ABOUT THE AUTHOR

T. Thorn Coyle has been arrested at least four times. Buy her a cup of tea or a good whisky and she'll tell you about it.

Author of the *The Witches of Portland*, the alt-history urban fantasy series *The Panther Chronicles*, the novel *Like Water*, and two story collections, her multiple non-fiction books include *Sigil Magic for Writers, Artists & Other Creatives*, and *Evolutionary Witchcraft*.

Thorn's work appears in many anthologies, magazines, and collections. She has taught magical practice in nine countries, on four continents, and in twenty-five states.

An interloper to the Pacific Northwest U.S., Thorn stalks city streets, writes in cafes, loves live music, and talks to crows, squirrels, and trees.

Connect with Thorn:
www.thorncoyle.com

ALSO BY T. THORN COYLE

Fiction Series

The Panther Chronicles

To Raise a Clenched Fist to the Sky

To Wrest Our Bodies From the Fire

To Drown This Fury in the Sea

To Stand With Power on This Ground

The Witches of Portland

By Earth

By Flame

By Wind

By Sea

By Moon

By Sun

By Dusk

By Dark

By Witches' Mark

Single Novels and Story Collections

Like Water

Alighting on His Shoulders

Break Apart the Stone

Anthologies

Fantasy in the City

Haunted

Witches Brew

The Faerie Summer

Stars in the Darkness

Fiction River: Justice

Fiction River: Feel the Fear

NON-FICTION

Evolutionary Witchcraft

Kissing the Limitless

Make Magic of Your Life

Sigil Magic for Writers, Artists & Other Creatives

Crafting a Daily Practice

CPSIA information can be obtained
at www.ICGtesting.com
Printed in the USA
FSHW022021061020
74557FS